Maggie Moore and the Secret School Diary

By Firna Rex Shaw

For Teigan

First Print Edition 2013
Copyright 2013

<u>Sunday, September 2nd</u>
<u>7pm</u>

It is seven o'clock in the evening and I'm squashed under my bed between tatty ted, an old Scrabble board and a pull-along turtle. Everything is so dusty it's making me want to sneeze, but I mustn't. I have to be very quiet, as I can't let Mum find me.

I have my new notebook and pen with me so that I can start my diary of the school year. School doesn't actually start until tomorrow but I wanted to write about why I have to hide. I have a problem you see, Mum has made me a school uniform dress out of an old tablecloth and she wants me to try it on, but I don't want to and I certainly don't want to wear it to school tomorrow. I wouldn't mind so much if it looked like a school dress. The colours are right, red and

3

white, but the check is far too big and it's shaped like a loose, lumpy bag.

In order to make this dress she drew two large strange potato shapes on the material, cut them out and sewed them together leaving little gaps for my head and arms to poke through. Worryingly, she also threw my two proper dresses from last term away saying they were too small.

She's coming. Shh.

1 Hour Later

8pm

She got me. She pretended she was calling the police to report a missing child. I crawled out covered in dust with the pull-along turtle tangled around my leg. I tried the 'dress' on and it looked terrible, it even had curry stains around the armholes. To try and cover it up, I've been secretly stretching my cardigan like mad. I've made it as big as I can so that it covers as much of the awful dress as possible, I just hope no one notices it when I get to school.

If it wasn't for the dress I'd be quite excited about tomorrow as we're going to have a new teacher. He's new so everyone is wondering what he'll be like. He's called Mr Burple and I expect him to be kind of purple, because of his name, but we'll have to wait and see.

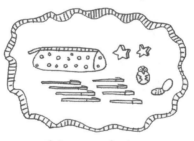

I've got everything ready in my new school bag:

a new pencil case

eight gel pens

four rubbers. (I am trying to collect rubbers, but I only have four so far: two stars, an owl

and an opening mobile phone rubber, the
highlight of the set.)

Mandy Smart has 97 rubbers in her collection!
(Well she did before the holiday. She probably
has more now.) She always goes on holiday to
the same hotel in America. The hotel is next
door to the world's biggest stationery shop. One
aisle in this shop has nothing but erasers
(rubbers) and, apparently, you can get a rubber
in the shape of ANYTHING you can think of!
Hmm.

Well, I can think of a toilet brush, guts, a
spider and a plaster covered in blood, but I
wouldn't want a rubber that looked like them. I

would quite like a recorder rubber that you could actually play, or a rubber in a rubber in a rubber where they all open up, a bit like a Russian doll, or a chocolate bar-shaped rubber that smells of chocolate.

I doubt I will ever go to America though. My family always go camping. We don't even go to the seaside... Oh no, we go on holiday to the middle of nowhere. Mum says it's nice to get away from everything, but I'm not so sure.

I go camping with Mum, Dad and my younger brother, Joppin. I usually share a tent room with Joppin, but he didn't want to last time and slept in the middle section (which should be a lounge).

Monday, September 3rd

I sat on a bench in the playground hoping no one would notice my dress, but of course everyone did. Holly ran over smiling and said it looked nice. Holly is always kind though; if I turned up in a dress made of turnips she'd say it was nice. Jake sneered and called me Raggie

7

Maggie. I told him it was a designer dress and really expensive. He looked impressed and ran off.

MR BURPLE

Luckily most people were talking about Mr Burple, which took the attention off me. Everyone was really excited about having a new teacher and it seems I wasn't the only one who had noticed that Mr Burple's name sounded a bit like purple. In fact, people were calling him purple Burple and making other jokes about his name.

The bell rang and we all ran in, pushing past each other to try and get a good seat. It didn't make any difference though as there was a sheet of paper on each desk with a name on it. I looked round for mine and found out that I was right at the front and next to Peter Potter. This was not good news.

Suddenly a strange man walked in. He was tall and thin with an enormous fluffy beard and moustache. He wore a bright yellow jumper and baggy brown corduroy trousers with leather knee patches.

We all sat quietly as he wrote 'MR BURPLE' on the whiteboard in enormous red letters. I could hear Jake trying not to laugh. He was shaking and holding his mouth shut. This made everyone else want to giggle and soon a wave of laughter rippled through the classroom. Mr Burple put his finger to his lips and the class became quiet again.

'Class,' his voice was serious and low. 'I know my name is Mr Burple, but please, no jokes about burps.'

This gave us all the brilliant idea of making jokes about burps which we did all playtime and half of lunchtime.

Example of a joke:

Q. *What colour is a burp?*

A. *Burple.*

That joke must have been told at least fifty times.

Mr Burple decided to start the day with us all making our own good work sheets. We had to decorate a sheet of paper with our name and a self-portrait. He said he was going to laminate them and put them on the wall.

9

'When your work is exceptional, you will get a special good work star.' He waved a sheet of shiny green stars in the air. 'Ten star stickers will earn you a dip in my lucky bag,' he said mysteriously, his green eyes twinkling like the stars.

We all got on with our sheets. My self-portrait was excellent. I drew myself standing on a small hill at the edge of the page and then added lots of detail... I even drew pockets and a zip on the jeans, and individual blades of grass on the hill.

Suddenly, I noticed Jake was hiding under the teacher's desk. He had a pencil in his hand and slowly, from under the desk, he moved the pencil up and slid it into Mr Burple's beard. The beard was so curly that the pencil stuck in and didn't move. Amazingly, Mr Burple didn't notice! Jake sneaked back to his seat. Everyone giggled and Jake got lots of pats on the back on his way. He was glowing with pride as he wrote 'Jake rocks' in 3D letters at the top of his good work sheet.

The pencil remained firmly lodged in the teacher's beard for quite a long time. Strangely, when we got back to the classroom after our playtime (and Mr Burple's tea break in the staff room), it was gone. But he didn't mention it at all.

All our good work sheets were stuck on the wall. The thought of a dip in the lucky bag is very exciting and I'm going to try and get a good work sticker as soon as possible. I thought I would have got one for my excellent self-portrait but it seems he doesn't give them out that easily.

At lunch, I sat with my group of friends: Holly Higgins, Mandy Smart and Sarah Dove. Mandy was showing us her three new rubbers from America.

A teacup rubber with removable tea.

A biscuit rubber with removable filling.

A parrot rubber. (Quentin, who Mandy sits next to, had accidentally broken off the beak. He told her not to worry as it now matches the others – it has a removable part.)

We all got our lunchboxes out. Holly, Sarah and I had yucky old ones, but Mandy had a brand new one from America. It was huge and bright red. It had a picture of a cartoon cat on the front and the words 'welcome to lunch' embossed in shiny gold lettering. Suddenly, we heard a woman's voice singing. We all looked round but we could only see Mrs Sad, the dinner lady, and she certainly wasn't singing.

'I hope you have fun,
I've packed you a bun,
And some sandwiches too,
I love you Hun.'
Sang the sweet voice.

Mandy looked mortified and snapped her lunchbox shut. The singing stopped.

'It's a recordable lunchbox,' she whispered. 'You can record a message on it. My mum must have recorded it this morning.'

'Brilliant,' I smiled. 'Let's see.'

She passed it over. I opened it and the singing started again.

'Nooo!' Mandy looked embarrassed.

I found a record button on the back of the lunchbox and pressed it.

'Hello, I'm Mr Carrot Stick. Please don't eat me.' I recorded before falling about laughing.

We all had a good play with the lunchbox. This meant we were ages in the lunchroom and hardly had any time to play outside.

When I got home I had this brilliant idea. I told Mum that I wasn't allowed to wear the dress to school, as it wasn't the proper uniform. Luckily, she believed me and is going to get me a proper one from a shop later this week. Phew. She said I could keep the tablecloth dress for parties and special occasions. I'm beginning to wonder which planet my mum lives on.

P.S. Holly is coming for tea on Friday.

Thursday, September 6th
TRUMPET

'Squeeeeeek' went the trumpet. I was trying to make my lips do the strange vibrating sound as instructed by the music teacher, Mr Stolliams, but I couldn't concentrate. I was too busy looking at what was next to me.

Quentin was sitting very near me holding his trumpet and playing quite a decent note. BUT, balanced carefully on his knee was a set of false teeth! There was a piece of plastic, shaped to fit in the top of his mouth with six teeth stuck on it! It was slimy and scary, and put me off my note. I had no idea that Quentin had false teeth. I didn't know that kids could have false teeth at all. His knee looked like it was smiling at me. I kept feeling my gaze moving towards the teeth as they glistened in the sun that streamed into the school hall. Quentin gave me a gappy smile and laughed. I looked away and tried to focus on making some sort of note come out of the trumpet. He picked up his teeth and moved them over as if he was about to put them on my knee! In a panic, I blew into my trumpet, producing my first ever proper note. Woo hoo.

So, how did I come to be doing trumpet? Well, there was a sheet of paper on the classroom wall. It said 'SIGN UP TO LEARN DANCE ROUTINES'. I put my name down. I was surprised that only Quentin had signed up but was confident that Holly, Mandy and Sarah would all want to do it too.

A few minutes later Mr Burple came into the room. Jake jumped up and raced over to the dance routines sign-up sheet and removed something that he had stuck over the title. The sheet now said 'TRUMPET LESSONS'.

'Splendid Maggie,' said Mr Burple as he examined the list. 'It's so great that you want to learn trumpet, such a wonderful instrument, so much history.'

'Yes,' I mumbled in shock.

He even gave Quentin and me a good work sticker, just for signing up for trumpet lessons! I was one of the first sticker owners in the class. I was very proud to have a green star, and was one tenth of the way toward a dip in the lucky dip bag. I was a little worried about the trumpet lessons though.

Mum was quite surprised when I returned home carrying a trumpet. 'Come on Maggie, play us a tune,' she said while miming playing the trumpet and marching around the room.

I had to get the trumpet out and managed to play one squeak. What was really annoying was that Joppin picked it up and immediately played about four notes. Joppin is much younger than me and in year two so he should, technically, be worse at everything than me. This was not good.

Anyway, I've found out that Mr Burple has always wanted to play the trumpet but missed his chance as a boy. He had come in at the end of our lesson and had a word with Mr Stolliams. It is all arranged. He is going to be learning along with Quentin and me. Lessons will be on Friday lunchtimes after lunch and before afternoon lessons. I think that playing beautifully could be a way to get more good work stickers so I started to practise as soon as I got in. It didn't sound that beautiful though. In fact I saw Mum give Dad a worried glance. Dad nodded as if he had a plan.

Friday, September 7th

Holly came for tea. We had pizza, dough balls and carrot sticks. We followed this with a very scrumptious chocolate cake for pudding. YUM. I love chocolate cake. If I could only eat one food for the rest of my life I think I would choose chocolate cake.

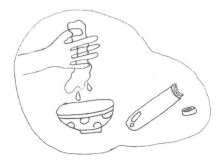

We played on my trampoline in the garden and then came in and inspected my slime collection. I have about ten different sorts of slimy and squidgy things. They're all in different plastic tubs; some are egg shaped, some test tube shape and some just boring cylinders. We poured each sort of gunge out of its tub and into a pudding bowl. We then squeezed the glorious goo through our fingers. After tea, we made up a dance routine; we even pretended we were slime as part of the dance. It was quite good.

I was in trouble for using all the pudding bowls and we had to wash them up. This was meant to be a punishment but it was actually great fun. We put loads of washing up liquid in the bowl and then, using straws, blew into the water and made masses of bubbles.

After Holly had gone home, I decided to practise my trumpet. I blew hard but all I could hear was a gurgling sound. I carefully turned the trumpet upside down and loads of water came out the end. I heard Joppin laughing from behind his door. I knew I'd have to get him back for this. After I'd emptied all the water out, I had a proper practice. I could play a few notes... but Mum kept coming in to tell me to keep the noise down. How am I meant to keep the noise down? It's a trumpet!

Wednesday, September 12th

TOP SECRET - TELL NO ONE ABOUT THIS!

Oh no, I may have caused an accident. It is very important that no one ever finds out about this. I could be in mega trouble.

I decided I had to get Joppin back for putting water in my trumpet, so this morning I had a brilliant idea, I decided to put some slime in one of his shoes. I waited until he was in the loo then opened up my slime collection and chose a clear, runny slime. I poured it into his shoe and then waited for the very funny moment when he noticed.

We were getting ready to go to school as usual and Joppin went to put his shoe on. I held my breath waiting for his shock and horror, but nothing happened.

He just put his shoe on as if everything was normal and got in the car. I thought nothing more of it until much later.

MATHS

'ALGERBRA' was written in big red letters on the board. Mr Burple was walking around the classroom making sure everyone was sitting neatly. We got our maths books out.

It turns out that algebra is where you use a letter to represent a number.

He rubbed ALGERBRA off the board and wrote.

$A+B=C$

$A = 11$

$B = 28$

$C =?$

What is the value of C?

Peter Potter, who I sit next to, shot his arm up before any of us had a chance to try and work it out. He was straining to hold his arm as high as possible, desperate to be picked. I suspected that he was after one of those green stars.

'Yes Peter?' Mr Burple said, picking up his red pen.

'Don't know,' said Peter.

'What is the value of C?'

'Don't know,' Peter repeated.

'Why is your hand up then?' Mr Burple sighed.

'Um, don't know.'

There was a long pause, by which time many others had come up with the answer.

'OK, we'll try someone else…. Quentin?'

'39,' said Quentin looking round and nodding smugly at everyone.

'Good,' said Mr Burple, writing the answer on the board then rubbing the whole sum out so he could write a new one.

Each time Mr Burple wrote a sum on the white board Peter Potter shot his hand up and said 'don't know'. It must have happened at least ten times. I was beginning to wish I sat next to Jake or Quentin; anything would be better than this.

Suddenly, someone saw an ambulance outside school. Everyone rushed to the window to see what was going on.

'Calm down children,' Mr Burple said, shutting the blinds. He looked worried. 'I'm sure it's nothing to worry about, carry on with your worksheets while I check something.' He hurried out of the classroom and everyone began talking, coming up with all sorts of ideas as to what may have happened.

After lunch there was an assembly. Mrs Foley, the head teacher, came in. She is a very neat-looking woman with short grey hair. She was wearing a black suit and red high heels.

'Good afternoon children.'

'Good afternoon Mrs Foley,' we all said. She then began to tell us about the accident that had happened.

In our school there's this special thing we do. We have to change out of our outside shoes and into pumps before coming into school. Each year has its own cloakroom where the shoe change takes place. It turns out that Mrs Simms, the year two teacher, had slipped on a strange slimy substance in the year two cloakroom and broken her leg. No one knew what the slimy substance was and Mrs Foley wanted to know if anyone had any information.

My blood ran cold. Could it be my slime? Could it have rubbed off Joppin's sock and ended up on the floor? I started shaking nervously. No one must ever know it might all be my fault.

Holly noticed my pale face. 'What's wrong Maggie?' she whispered.

'I just don't like hearing about accidents,' I replied quietly.

Holly linked my arm. 'I don't like to think about it either.'

Thoughts were racing through my mind. I wondered if Joppin had noticed the slimy sock. If he hadn't then I had to get the sock before he did, so I could destroy the evidence.

The rest of the day was a nightmare. All I could think about was the slime. All I could wonder was whether I'd be found out? Would I go to prison? I didn't know.

In the car on the way home Joppin was acting normally and I was pretty sure he didn't know about the slime. I wasn't acting normally at all. I was staring at his foot trying to figure out how to get his sock off without him noticing.

When we got home he kicked his shoes into the corner of the hall and I could see his sock, yes it was slimy. He sat on the sofa and put on the telly.

'Wrestling time!' I said, which surprised him enormously as I have never ever wrestled with him before. He looked at me suspiciously. I leapt on him pretending to be trying to pin him down while all the time I was trying to remove his sock with my toes.

'What are you doing?' he gasped as he struggled.

'New game,' I said, my big toe now hooked into the top of the sock. Joppin started to wrestle back and then, after about ten minutes, I got the sock. As soon as I had it I bundled it into my pocket and was gone. I sneaked into the garden and pushed it well down into the wheelie bin – phew. No one would ever know now. I gave his shoe a quick wipe round with a piece of kitchen roll and finally sat down to relax.

It had all been so stressful. It was lovely to lie on the sofa and let the tension ebb away. Joppin had vanished so I changed the TV to channel 70 ready to watch my favourite show about designing kids' bedrooms. I breathed out a huge sigh of relief.

'WRESTLING TIME!' shouted Joppin as he ran in and jumped on me. I had to wrestle him for fifteen minutes and I missed half of my show. Still, at least I was no longer in danger of being found out.

Monday, September 24th

I got a good work sticker today for helping to clear up after art. This means I only have eight to get before my dip in the lucky bag. Hooray!

DAD

I haven't told you this before but my dad is really into making things. When I got back from school last Thursday he started acting strangely. First, he measured how tall I was then he drew different sized circles in chalk on the drive and made me stand in them while he made notes. He looked really excited but whenever I asked what it was for he just told me to wait and see.

Dad has this shed in the garden. He calls it his workshop but it's actually just a shed full of junk. He keeps anything that he thinks may be useful for one of his inventions in there. The day after the measuring I saw him carrying four full bin bags into the shed. The last bag had a rip in it and I could see a load of old egg boxes. It was very strange.

Over the years, he's made some odd things.

A few of my dad's crazy inventions:

- A body suit covered in sponges. (We actually had to wear this to the park in case we fell over.)

- Gloves and hat set tied together with elastic string. Whenever I moved my arms the hat got pulled further onto my head. Once, the hat got pulled on so tightly I couldn't get it off. Dad had to pull like mad to remove it. (I had a bald patch for three months.)

- Shoes with loads of small springs on the bottom. Dad said it would make us feel like we were 'walking on air'. It didn't feel like walking on air, it felt like walking on lots of small springs.

- A portable garden. This was a tray full of plants that we would take out with us, so we could always have that garden feeling wherever we were. It had wheels and a rope handle. We took it to the beach, we took it to the shops and once we even took it to the cinema. This was especially silly as it was dark so we couldn't see it.

Dad is convinced that sometime soon he will come up with a brilliant idea that everyone will want. He's got this dream that one day he'll be a famous inventor.

Wednesday, September 26th

When I got back from school yesterday, Dad announced that his latest invention was ready. He had put it in my room and I had to go in blindfolded so that it would be a surprise. He got his phone out ready to film my reaction and followed me as I stumbled up the stairs with my blindfold on. Joppin raced up behind us, curious to see what was going on. I went into my room and Dad got Joppin to whip the blindfold off while he filmed. It was then that I saw the strangest sight of my life.

It was a cylinder-shaped box, which was a bit taller than me, with a door in the side. Egg box trays were glued all over it, covering the whole surface.

'What is it?'

'Welcome to your totally soundproofed trumpet practice pod,' Dad said proudly, 'sticking egg boxes on things makes them soundproof you know. You can practice in there and no one will hear a thing.'

'Oh,' I said.

It looked like it would be quite cramped and dark inside, but I went in so as not to hurt Dad's feelings. I could move about a bit but it wasn't nice and I was bit miffed that he didn't want to hear my practising.

'Now, lets test the soundproofing,' said Dad eagerly as he handed me the trumpet. It was then that we all realized that there was a major problem with the design. A person could fit in OK, but it was too small for a person playing a trumpet. There was only one thing to do. We had to remove one of the egg boxes, make a round hole in the box, and stick the end of the trumpet out of the 'pod'. This made the whole thing pointless but I played a tune, Little Fly (only one note), while Dad filmed.

I knew it wasn't going to be useful long term because I had to play in the dark and couldn't see the music. Luckily I knew Little Fly off by heart so Dad didn't realize. In fact, Little Fly is the only tune I can play off by heart.

So now I have a big egg box mess in my room and there isn't a lot I can do about it.

Friday, October 5th

I now have four good work stickers, which means that I am four tenths of my way towards getting a dip in the lucky bag. I got number three for playing Little Fly perfectly, and number four for helping Holly when she fell and cut her knee at playtime.

Most people have one, two or three stars. Holly only has one but Quentin has nine! He keeps showing off that he is going to be the first to get a dip. It is so annoying. I don't know how he managed to get so many as Mr Burple hardly ever gives them out. Even Mr Burple looked shocked when Quentin said he only had one more to get. I really hope Quentin doesn't get a dip anytime soon as he will go on and on about it and it will be so annoying.

Today we had a trumpet lesson. I've got used to Quentin's false teeth looking at me now and managed to train myself not to look back at them. I certainly didn't look at them today. Something far more interesting was going on. Mr Burple was sitting in between us with his trumpet, but he was struggling because his beard was stuck in his cardigan zip at the top. He clearly didn't want anyone to notice, so he just pretended he was looking down all the time.

Mr Stolliams didn't realize and kept telling Mr Burple to hold his trumpet up more. Mr Stolliams is very serious and scary and I could tell Mr Burple was becoming flustered. The zip of his cardigan was being pulled forward as he tried to raise his trumpet a little. We played Little Fly a few times and were given a new song to practice at home. I did feel a bit sorry for Mr Burple and wondered if I should offer to cut his beard so he'd be free. But if I did that then he would know that I had noticed, and I got the feeling that he didn't want anyone to notice.

I needn't have worried though as after lunch I saw that he was looking up again. I also noticed a large tuft of beard left in his zip.

After lunch, Quentin suddenly had ten green stickers. No one seemed to remember him getting star number ten, not even Mr Burple. But Quentin insisted it was true, even going up to his chart and counting to ten while pointing at each sticker. Mr Burple got out his dark purple velvet bag, which was very smart with a gold cord and the letters B.B. sewn onto it in shiny material. I wondered what B.B. stood for? Perhaps Burple's Bag or Burple's Boogers (I hope not)?

Quentin made a big thing of going up to the front. He waved at everyone as he walked forward like he was about to be made king. Once at the front, he turned to the class and bowed before turning to look in the bag. He spent a long time rummaging around before finally choosing his item. He took it out, hidden in his hand, and put it straight in his pocket. Everyone was dying to know what was it was but he wouldn't say.

'Tell you at playtime,' he said as he sat down.

We had a creative writing lesson. I wrote a story about a cat that could stand up and look through letterboxes. I thought it was quite good. I hoped I'd get a green star. (I didn't.)

At afternoon play a huge crowd gathered round Quentin. Everyone was asking him what he got and what else was in the bag.

'I can't show you, but it's a magic item,' Quentin said, enjoying all the attention. 'The bag is full of items for spells and magic. I think Mr Burple is a wizard.' Most of us looked doubtful but a few of the children looked like they believed him.

'Well what magic item did you get?' asked Jake.

'A rabbit's foot, as white as snow and as soft as fur. It's very special and I must never show it to anyone. It will bring me amazing powers, so don't make me angry.'

He refused to show anyone the magic rabbit's foot, but everyone was talking about it and a few more people began to think it might be true. I was more determined than ever to get a dip in that bag.

Monday, October 8th

Peter Potter was at it again today. His hand went up so many times I began to think he was fanning me. Each time it happened Mr Burple asked for his answer and Peter replied 'don't know'. Mr Burple was usually quite calm but I could see that he was starting to tire of the whole thing.

The first lesson was about Ancient Egypt. We had to make pyramids out of yellow card and draw bricks on them. Mine was quite good and I even did shading to make the bricks look more realistic. The hardest bit was figuring out the shapes to cut out of card. I thought I'd get a good work star. (I didn't.)

At lunchtime, Quentin came and sat at our table. He doesn't usually sit with us but a French child, who was visiting someone in year six, had sat in his usual place. We were quite pleased though as it gave us a chance to talk about the lucky dip bag.

'Have you done anything with your magic rabbit's foot?' asked Holly.

'Oh yes,' said Quentin

'Well what?' I asked.

Quentin leaned in, his voice becoming a whisper. 'Last night, I did a few basic spells with it... I turned a goldfish to stone.'

'No, please tell me you didn't,' said Sarah, gasping and putting her hands over her mouth in horror.

'It was annoying me, all that swishing about in the water. Best not to annoy me now,' Quentin said as he opened his lunchbox.

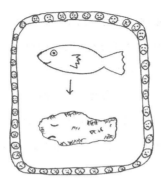

I was doubtful but decided to keep an open mind.

Suddenly, Mandy pointed in Quentin's lunchbox. We all looked, stunned. There, hidden under a large lettuce leaf was a sheet of shiny green stickers, the exact sort that Mr Burple used on the good work sheets.

'You've got your own stickers! You cheated!' said Mandy, her mouth wide open.

Quentin looked panicked but then became calm again as a plan formed in his mind. He pulled out the stickers.

'Yes, I got the stickers from a shop, and used them on my sheet. But...' he paused for effect. 'I'm going to eat the evidence.'

He put the stickers in his mouth, chewed them awkwardly for quite a while and swallowed them. We all stared in shock.

'Don't bother telling anyone, no one will believe you, you'll just look jealous and pathetic,' he said and then shut his lunchbox and left the room.

'I can't believe it,' I said.

'And we can't even prove it,' said Sarah sadly.

'We can,' Mandy's eyes sparkled as she opened her lunchbox and we heard Quentin's confession. 'I recorded it all on the recordable lunchbox.'

We all laughed and high-fived. It was decided that Sarah would tell Mr Burple and after lunch she took the lunchbox straight to the staffroom.

At lunchtime play we saw Quentin smugly talking about the rabbit's foot. On and on he went, threatening to turn kids to stone. Some of the year one and two kids were crying as he chased them round the playground, chanting spells. Eventually the bell went and we all filed in. We were going to draw the River Nile on big pieces of card then sit our pyramids near it, all the art equipment was out ready. Mr Burple was sitting at the front, his purple velvet bag on his desk. He had written 'THE NILE' on the whiteboard.

I was quite nervous about what might happen if Mr Burple mentioned the cheating. Would Quentin know we'd told on him? Would he turn us to stone? I was quite sure the magic thing was made up but still felt a bit funny in my tummy. I looked at Mandy, she looked double nervous, as she sits next to Quentin. She moved her seat as far away from his as possible and was looking out of the window whistling silently. When everyone noticed the purple bag they began checking the sheets to see if anyone had ten stickers. But no one was anywhere near. There was lots of whispering about what was going on. Suddenly Mr Burple banged his hand on the desk.

'There has been a severe case of cheating in this class,' Mr Burple said sounding serious.

Quentin started rolling a pen between his fingers faster and faster.

'Quentin, put that pen down,' he pointed at Quentin who quickly dropped the pen. 'I know you have used your own stickers. It doesn't matter how I know but I do know.'

Quentin's mouth dropped open.

'No, um I wouldn't do that,' he stammered.

Mr Burple stood up.

'Please come and put the item you took from the lucky dip bag back in the bag now,' Mr Burple said calmly.

'Um, can I just hang onto it until I really have ten stickers?' asked Quentin quietly.

'Come here and give me the item,' demanded Mr Burple.

Everyone sat in silence waiting to see what would happen.

'Can I pay for it then?' asked Quentin sheepishly.

Mr Burple looked near purple and put his hands on his hips.

'Quentin,' he began, his voice booming, 'come and return the pink butterfly rubber you took from my bag now.'

Everyone started laughing. Jake had tears of laughter streaming down his face. Quentin went bright red, ran up to the front and got something out his pocket. Mr Burple held the out his hand. Quentin gave him the item and ran back to his seat. Mr Burple held up a pink butterfly rubber. Everyone was giggling and chattering about it. Quentin sat down, not looking at anyone.

'Silence!' said Mr Burple. We all went quiet.

'Thank you Quentin, and no more cheating please, you will have to start collecting again from zero.'

Wednesday, October 10th

Quentin is still looking embarrassed about the sticker and 'rabbit's foot' incident. He said that Mr Burple did a spell that turned the foot into a rubber. No one believes him. He's gone a bit quiet in class, which is a relief. I just wish Peter Potter would go quiet too and stop saying 'don't know' all the time. I told Mr Burple to ask the class 'what do you say if you don't know something?'

This would mean that Peter could be right for once. I thought my idea was brilliant but Mr Burple just said that he would deal with it in his own way.

SCHOOL TRIP ALERT

Something quite exciting happened today. We found out that we are going to be going on a school trip. We will be walking to Honeybee Farm. It's not a proper farm. It's a sort of farm attraction. Everyone sits on hay bales and plays with the guinea pigs. I think there are a few pigs and a maze too. It's really close to my house and I've been heaps of times with my family, but it will be fun going with the whole class. The trip will be on Monday, November 12th. (There are no bees.)

Thursday, October 11th

We had a special assembly today. After we'd sung a few songs Mrs Foley came in and stood at the front of the hall. She took a deep breath and started talking about the importance of honesty. Everyone was looking at Quentin, waiting for a reaction, but he looked ahead and didn't flinch. She said honesty was important in all areas of life.

'It is better to lose than to cheat,' she said and looked at us dramatically. Quentin started fidgeting. She talked about being honest about our feelings. 'A problem shared will bring relief and support.' She nodded slowly for effect. 'Asking, when you don't know will help others to help you.' She raised her arms in the air. 'It shows great strength to say 'I don't know', never be afraid of those words.' She punched the air, smiling hard. 'This is why I became a teacher, to pass on wisdom like this. Now get up and seize the day.' We all filed out.

At lunchtime play Holly showed me her new hand warmer. Her mum had brought it back from Austria, when she went on a skiing holiday with her friends. It's an orangey brown 15cm tube of really soft fake fur. It hangs around her neck on a string and you put your hands in either end. We all had a go and it was really warm. I didn't want to take my hands out. I wish my mum was the sort of glamorous mum who went skiing and brought back fantastic presents.

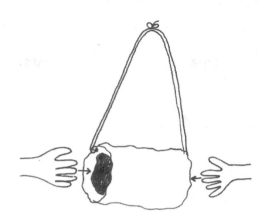

My mum is a slightly strange lady who runs an eBay shop from the spare room. She sells vintage clothes and the house is overrun with bags and boxes of old, out-of-fashion garments, which make the house smell a bit musty. She also likes gardening, and grows vegetables, oh and she listens to Radio 4 a lot.

MATHS LESSON

In the afternoon we had maths.

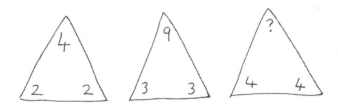

Mr Burple drew these triangles on the board. Of course, Peter Potter put his hand up within a millisecond. Mr Burple ignored him so he put his hand up higher, straining and saying 'me, me, me'.

Mr Burple looked him in the eye. 'Peter?' he said, just a glimmer of hope in his voice.

'... don't know,' said Peter.

Mr Burple looked ready to explode. He turned around and dramatically rubbed out the triangles. His wiping motion was swift and cross. He then wrote in HUGE letters right across the whiteboard...

NO ONE IS ALLOWED TO SAY 'DON'T KNOW' IN THIS CLASS!

He turned to face the class, breathing out his frustration and squeezing his hands. We all stared nervously not knowing what would happen next.

Suddenly Mrs Foley came into the room. We all became silent and still as she looked at the board in horror.

'You'd better come outside with me,' she said sharply.

They walked out and we could hear Mr Burple apologizing. He then came back in on his own and silently rubbed the message off the board.

Friday, October 12th

There was a trumpet lesson today. We had started learning slightly harder tunes and Mr Stolliams said we might be able to play a song in the Christmas concert. He is going to speak to Mrs Rizla about it.

Mrs Rizla is the year one teacher. It is usually Mrs Simms who does the concert but she is off with a broken leg (eek!). Apparently Mrs Rizla jumped at the chance to do the concert. She said it was her dream and she had some amazing ideas.

'Us playing in the concert,' beamed Mr Burple. 'Oh, what an opportunity.'

Mrs Simms, the year two teacher, came to visit today. She had a huge pot on her leg and hobbled about on crutches. She was going to be off for another six weeks. I felt guilty but she said she's been doing loads of reading and has been enjoying her time off, so I feel a bit better about it now.

Another highlight of the day was that Holly let me use her hand warmer all play time.

Wednesday, October 24th

I practised my trumpet last night. Dad was upstairs so I had to stand in the soundproof practice pod with the trumpet sticking out of the hole. I tried to play Little Fly. I blew and blew but made the quietest notes I've ever heard, and my cheeks nearly cracked open under the pressure. Because I was in the dark and couldn't see the end of the trumpet, it was ages before I realised the reason it was almost unplayable. There was a marshmallow stuck in the end.

I assumed it was Joppin. I would normally try and get him back for something like this but because of what happened last time, I decided not to. I got the marshmallow out with a fork. I tried eating it, but it tasted disgusting and I had to spit it out.

CHRISTMAS CONCERT ALERT

At school today, Mrs Rizla told us that the Christmas concert was being planned. Turns out we're doing 'Nursery Rhymes at Christmas'. We all groaned when we were told. Everyone was saying how babyish it was but Mrs Rizla told us that she'd had this idea for years and it was going to be totally brilliant.

I agree that it is babyish but I am determined to get an actual proper part this year. Last year, I was a camel's post. Yes, that's right a camel's post... the post that a camel is tied too.

A camel was a pretty rubbish part so you can imagine how I felt about being a camel's post. Needless to say, the post didn't speak. My only moment of glory was when the rope was tied around my waist. Jake, the camel's owner (good part), tied it so tight I bent over, causing everyone to laugh. Mrs Simms didn't laugh though, she took it all very seriously and said that I had ruined the illusion of being a post – great. Perhaps Mrs Rizla doing the concert would be more fun?

We were informed that over the next two weeks they were deciding who would do which parts. I decided to practise very loud clear talking.

When I got home I immediately began practising my loud talking. I stood at the bottom of the garden talking to mum who stood at the back door.

'I am umm,' I desperately tried to remember some characters from nursery rhymes but was finding it hard. 'Jack Horner!' I shouted.
Mum laughed. This encouraged me.

'I sit in a corner,' I bellowed.

Suddenly a cross voice came from next-door's garden. 'Well sit in a corner and be quiet.'

I ran in, deciding to practise in my pod instead of the garden.

THE FARM COUNTDOWN HAS BEGUN

There are less than three weeks to go until the farm trip. Mum is taking me to buy some wellies on Saturday. Woo hoo, diddly doo!

Friday, November 2nd

This morning we had PSHE, which stands for 'personal, social and health education.' This is a lesson where we talk about things like being healthy, dealing with arguments, problems…. Stuff like that.

'HOW I STAY CLEAN AND HEALTHY' was written on the board in large red letters. I decided to show Mr Burple how loud and clearly I could speak.

'Can anyone give me an example of a way to keep clean and healthy?' he asked.

I shot my hand up, nearly as quickly as Peter. Luckily I was picked.

'Wear clean clothes,' I bellowed. It came out much louder than expected and kind of sounded like I was shouting at Mr Burple. Everyone cracked up. Only when Mr Burple looked down did I notice the stain on his trousers.

'Not you,' I gulped, 'I mean everybody.'

That kind of made it worse. He walked around so his trousers were hidden behind a desk.

'Peter?' he asked, obviously trying to move the focus away from his trousers.

'Don't know,' Peter said.

Oh dear.

We had a trumpet lesson just before lunch. Turns out that we are going to be playing 'Ten Green Bottles' in the concert. Mrs Rizla said that she knew it wasn't technically a nursery rhyme but it was OK, as it would give ten children a good part. So this means that Mrs Rizla thinks that being a green bottle, and no doubt having to fall over, is a good part. I'm beginning to worry.

The afternoon lesson was all about nursery rhymes. (I guess this is why Mrs Rizla was sitting in.) We all had to think of a rhyme and write it down. Then we took it in turns to read them out in front of the class. This was my big chance to shine. When it was my turn I went up to the front, trying to look really confident. I read out Little Miss Muffet.

In case you don't know it... it goes like this.

Little Miss Muffet,

sat on a tuffet

Eating her curds and whey.

Along came a spider

who sat down beside her

And frightened Miss Muffet away.

While I was reading, I noticed that Mrs Rizla and Mr Burple were talking. They looked pleased and nodded to each other. Then they wrote something down in their concert notebook. I was pretty sure I would get to be Miss Muffet and, when I asked Mr Burple if I had a part, he actually said, 'Yes, we are going to give you a really funny part.'

I couldn't concentrate for the rest of the lesson. I was too busy imaging what my Miss Muffet part was going to be like. I imagined...

1. Me eating pretend curds and whey. (Which would actually be chocolate cake, as curds and whey sounds disgusting.)

2. Me talking to the spider, perhaps arguing about who was going to sit where.

3. The chase scene which would be hilarious, perhaps I could even have the spider chasing me around the audience.

Yes, I will make Little Miss Muffet really amusing. I'll probably be the star of the show.

I was so excited when I got home. I told Mum, Dad and Joppin. Mum rang Grandma, Granddad, Uncle Jon, Auntie Sue and Dad's old friend Jim Bob. Everyone was so pleased. I practised my part in front of the family and they all laughed, as I was so funny. Joppin even pretended to be the spider so I could practise the chase. This went on all over the house and garden. I wonder what I will be wearing? I imagine it will probably be a funny dress with large puffed sleeves. I insisted that everyone called me Muffet for the rest of the day.

Friday, November 9th

The farm trip in three days! I've got my new wellies. They are purple with a black trim.

Today at school we talked about the trip and Mr Burple told us that there is a webcam at the farm.

'What's a webcam?' asked Jake.

'Well,' said Mr Burple, 'There is a camera on the farm roof. It's filming the farm garden all the time, day and night. If you go to the website you can watch the film and see what it happening at any given moment.'

He turned on the interactive whiteboard screen and opened up the farm website and eventually found the webcam page which showed the field behind the farm barn.

On the webcam we could see the entrance to the maze and a pig wandering about. I wonder if the pig ever wanders into the maze and gets lost? That would be quite sad. There were also two pigsties and a guinea pig run, which is just a large wooden box with hay. Oh, there were also a few picnic tables. I hope we aren't going to have to sit outside for lunch; it's only three degrees today and I can't see it getting much warmer before tomorrow.

Monday, November 12th
FARM TRIP

Woo hoo!

Farm trip day! I put my new wellies on at 8am. Mum insisted I tuck my trousers into my boots but it looked ridiculous so I untucked them as soon as I got to school.

Mr Burple told us all to find a partner (I picked Holly). We then walked, in what he called a 'Human Bus Formation', (no comment), to the farm. Let's just say that the constant 'honking' of the bus horn by the girls at the front wasn't that funny after the sixteenth time.

Once there, we all traipsed into the field and waved at the webcam, which was perched on a corner of the roof. Jake was messing around doing some strange dancing. He said that because of the webcam he could become an Internet sensation. I doubt this as when we looked at the webcam page at school it showed 'number of visitors to this page since 2006 – 12'. I suddenly saw Mr Burple grab Jake who was busy pretending to pull his trousers down, much to his friend's amusement. Oh dear. Luckily, it was unlikely anyone would have been looking at the webcam at that moment.

Mrs Honeybee, the 'farmer', ushered us all into the barn. This was good as it was freezing outside and there were some large red heaters hanging from the barn ceiling.

We all sat on hay bales and Mrs Honeybee read out a plan of what we would be doing:

Playing with guinea pigs

Putting the guinea pigs away and counting them

Outside play

Lunch

Looking at the pigs

Drawing the pigs (obviously just to fill up time as there isn't much to do)

Questions and answers (I could sense some long silences coming on)

Quick outside play

Leave

Mrs Honeybee then went to get the guinea pigs out of a large wooden cage. She started handing them out. They were so cute and furry and I was pleased with the brown and white one I was given. I passed it from hand to hand and tickled it under the chin. Holly put her orangey one in her hand warmer and when it popped its head out you could hardly see where the hand warmer ended and the guinea pig began.

Quentin had about five guinea pigs on him. He said that animals just loved him and wanted to be near him. He said he gave off good vibes. But I could see a carrot sticking out of his pocket.

I needed the toilet and put my hand up.

'Mrs Honeybee, is there a loo?' I asked.

'Yes my dear,' she replied, 'out of the barn door, across the field in a yellow hut.' She smiled, taking the guinea pig off me and cuddling it against her chin. 'Hello Barbara,' she said to it. 'Oh,' she added, 'be very careful going out; don't let any guinea pigs out of the barn.'

On my way back from the loo I opened the barn door very carefully. However, as soon as it was open an orangey brown guinea pig ran out at high speed. It shot across the field and vanished. I entered the barn feeling horrified, luckily no one had noticed.

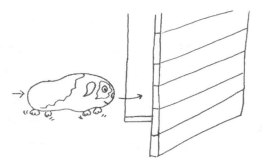

After about an hour of guinea pig play, Mrs Honeybee said to put all the cuddly rodents back in the cage so she could count them.

OH NO!

I quickly told Holly what had happened and begged her to let me put her hand warmer in the cage so it would look like the missing animal. Holly reluctantly agreed after I promised to find the escaped guinea pig and swap them back later.

We buried the hand warmer half under some hay in the corner of the cage so that it looked just like a sleeping guinea pig. Mrs Honeybee did the count and smiled.

'All counted, lovely,' she said before opening the door for outside play.

Holly and I breathed a huge sigh of relief. During outside play we were busy looking for the lost creature, but we couldn't find it anywhere. Later on we had lunch and did our pig drawings. Mine was quite good, I wondered if I might get a star. (I didn't.) Holly was sad about her hand warmer but I promised I'd sort it out, even if I had to come back on Saturday.

At the end of the day we had a quick last play. Mr Burple then announced that it was nearly time for the Human Bus to return to school. It was just as everyone was getting into formation that Mr Burple realised that Jake was missing. After looking everywhere and calling out twenty times, it was decided that he must be lost in the maze. We offered to go in and look for him but Mr Burple said there was no way he was risking losing anyone else or himself. We all had to wait for ages while a fire engine with a huge ladder came. A fireman on top of the ladder was raised into the air overlooking the maze. Jake was found reading a comic close to the entrance and Mr Burple was furious all the way back. We were one hour late and all the parents were complaining to Mrs Foley.

On the way home, I devised a plan for finding the guinea pig. I will sneak into the farm tomorrow after tea. It closes at 5 o'clock so there will be no one around. I will then find the guinea pig, keep it at home for a bit then go to the farm on Saturday when it's open to the public, and switch the found guinea pig for the hand warmer... simple.

Tuesday, November 13th

Last night, in bed, I started to feel a bit bad about the lost guinea pig. I hope the little creature is OK. This worry has made me even more determined to find it. I've been thinking about my plan, (now called 'Project Find the Guinea Pig'), and I've realised there's a major problem with it. I could be seen on the webcam! I need a disguise. Luckily I have one right here in my room! Yes, I am turning my soundproof practice pod into a... tree! I am then going to take it down to the farm after tea, once the farm is shut. If anyone happens to look at the webcam while I'm there they will never know it's me. It will just look like a tree. Genius.

So I've been painting my practice pod brown to make it look trunkish. I was just in the middle of painting it when Dad came in. He looked down at me as I crouched, paint brush in hand.

'Oh precious, you're decorating it,' he gulped, looking so pleased.

'Yeah, I love it so much I'm making it look extra good with paint,' I said, brushing away.

'That is great, this is the first time one of my inventions has really been appreciated.' He wiped a tear of joy from his eye and then helped me finish it off.

TONIGHT IS THE NIGHT.

Tuesday, November 13th
6.30pm

Well, after tea I said I was doing homework in my room, but I actually sneaked the pod out of the front door. I got some branches and leaves from the garden and headed for the farm. It was hard to see where I was going even though I was shining my torch out of the hole in the box.

Luckily there was hardly anyone about. I did see a man but I stood motionless at the edge of the pavement and he walked straight past (rather quickly).

I got to the farm and climbed over the wall. (Not easy in the pod.) I scuttled around the field in the tree costume. I was staggering about, tripping over things erratically. I was shining the torch about randomly. I went in the maze. I looked in the pigsties. I hunted under the picnic tables but found nothing.

After about an hour of stumbling around I accepted defeat and went home. I got back into my room at around 8pm, just as Mum came to see how the homework was going. Phew!

I really hope the little guinea pig is coping well with its life outside the cage.

Wednesday, November 14th

Holly is still annoyed with me about the hand warmer and I'm still worried about the guinea pig. I really wish I'd just told Mrs Honeybee about the missing animal straight away as it feels too late to tell her now. I don't know why I didn't say anything. I just kind of panicked. I'm going to go to the farm on Saturday for another look.

Thursday, November 15th

OH MY GOSH!

OH MY GIDDY AUNT!

BLIMEY!

I am an Internet star (kind of).

I was in the lounge with Mum, Dad and Joppin last night. We were watching the local news.

'And the latest Internet sensation started right here in our area at Honeybee Farm,' said the newsreader.

I looked up from my book and they were showing webcam footage...of me! There I was in my tree outfit, staggering about the field and disappearing into the maze.

'The website has had 10,000 hits but the strange walking tree has not been seen again,' the lady said.

Dad looked at me; I looked at Dad and froze. Dad raised an eyebrow in a knowing way. I went red.

'Looks just like your practice pod with twigs in it,' said Mum.

'Yeah, it does a bit,' I said casually.

Luckily the news moved on to babies at the local hospital, which Mum found very interesting.

Today at school, everyone was talking about the famous farm. Mr Burple even left the website with the webcam on all day in case the tree came back. I wondered if I should go to the farm as a tree again, to keep the fans happy, but decided not to. There could be people waiting there, ready to catch the tree.

It's kind of good to be famous, but I'm the only one who knows it's me, which takes the shine off it slightly.

CHRISTMAS CONCERT UPDATE

The green bottles for the Christmas play have been decided. We played our trumpets as some boys pretending to be bottles sang and fell over. The rest of the parts are being announced on Monday. Not that I need to wait, after all I already know my part. Waa Hoo!

We got the Christmas concert dates last week, December 10th, 11th and 12th. Mum has booked hotels for the relatives. Mum and Dad and five other relatives (as well as Jim Bob – Dad's old friend) are coming.

I hope the guinea pig is OK. It did have quite long fur so hopefully it's not too cold. I've been thinking about it a lot today and feel terrible for not telling Mrs Honeybee it went missing. I have decided that, if I don't find it at the farm tomorrow, I'm going to have to tell her about what happened, even if it means getting into trouble. Eeeeeeek.

Saturday, November 17th

I went to the farm this morning (normal clothes). I was nervous and my feet felt like jelly. I had a look around outside, but the guinea pig was nowhere to be seen, so I went inside to look for Mrs Honeybee. It was very busy in the barn, but Mrs Honeybee recognized me and rushed straight over.

'Oh, have you come for your hand warmer?' she asked.

'Yes,' I said hopefully.

'I saw you playing with it and then I found it in the cage,' she said as she went off to get it.

'Great news,' I stammered as she returned, 'um I need to talk to you about something.' I looked down, unable to look her in the eye. 'I think a guinea pig may be missing.' My ears went all tingly as I waited for her reply.

'Oh yes, fluffy Kevin, yes he escaped on the day of your school visit,' she said.

'Oh, you know about it?' I replied, my whole body starting to shake. I looked up and was surprised to see that she didn't look angry at all.

'Yes, but luckily we found him the next day, he'd made a little nest under a bush,' she paused and looked at me, 'but I'm really pleased you came and told me.' She touched my arm and I felt a few tears of relief form in my eyes.

I smiled all the way home and rang Holly straight away.

I now officially have NO PROBLEMS. It is such a nice feeling to have absolutely nothing to worry about. I can't stop smiling. Life is looking rather good.

I feel a song coming on...

Number of problems equals zero.
Number of problems equals none.
Number of problems equals zero,
All my problems are g...g...gone.

Friday, November 23rd

I had a trumpet lesson with Mr Stolliams today.
We played 10 green bottles over and over again.
It's beginning to sound quite respectable now, but
it makes the lessons extremely boring. My Burple
is very excited. He keeps saying that he's always
wanted to play a musical instrument in public.

'Who would have thought that being a teacher
would help me realise my dream of playing
trumpet on stage,' he beamed.

After lunch the list of who was what in the
Christmas concert was put on the pin board in the
classroom. Everyone crowded round. I didn't
bother looking until...

'I'm Miss Muffet!' Claire shouted.

I couldn't believe it and elbowed my way
through the crowds. I scanned the list,
gobsmacked.

Miss Muffet – Claire Bagshaw

The Tuffet – Maggie Moore
Green Bottle 1 – Jake Turbolt
Green Bottle 2 – Greg Powers
... and so on.

What? I AM A TUFFET? I went quiet, in panic mode. What is a tuffet? All I know for sure is that Miss Muffet sits on one. I looked at big Claire and started to worry.

I just know I won't be able to tell Mum. All I can do is hope that the tuffet is a really, really good part.

Friday, November 23rd (later)

Just looked up Tuffet on the Internet. Not the best news I'm afraid.

Tuffet – a small grassy hill or clump of grass.

Oh no, what are the chances of a clump of grass talking and cracking jokes. And a chase scene seems very unlikely now. Worse news is Mum still thinks I'm Miss Muffet and I can't bring myself to tell her I'm not.

When I sat down in the lounge earlier tonight Mum sat down next to me. She put her arm around me, pulling me in.

'Well done for getting such a good part in the play darling,' she said.

'Just shows that all that time spent practising your clear and loud talking worked.'

'Yes,' added Dad. 'Put in the hard work to get the results; you've made me and your mum so proud.'

My heart dropped and I said nothing.

P.S. Joppin is going to be Humpty Dumpty, the narrator, and star of the show!

Monday, November 26th

Today, we were working on the concert. The ten green bottle outfits are ready and quite good. Bo Peep's sheep have been gluing white fluff onto white body suits. I just sat around doodling. Then Mrs Rizla appeared at the classroom door.

'Maggie, come into the corridor with me please,' she shouted.

I went out.

'Now,' she said, 'could you roll into a ball shape on the floor and curl up as much as possible,' she pointed to the floor, 'be as small as you can be.'

I curled up small and she tried placing a variety of wooden boxes over me. In the end she found one that just covered me.

'Great,' she smiled. 'This is your costume.' She handed me the box. 'In that cupboard you'll find a roll of fake grass, just glue some on and you're ready. Easy eh?'

I blinked to hold back the tears as I went off with my box. I spent the next hour gluing a sheet of fake grass onto it. Holly was the owl from the Owl and the Pussycat. She was making an amazing owl mask with real feathers. It looked really good.

'Hey, good tuffet,' Holly said kindly, tapping my box.

I nodded and began making two eyeholes in the box so I could at least see out a bit.

Later on, Mrs Rizla came to see how we were getting on.

'Oh Maggie, you've left two holes in yours,' she said and pointed at my eyeholes. 'But don't worry, I've got just the thing.' She then got two corks out of her pocket and glued them into the

holes. Oh no, squashed and in the dark –
nightmare!

Tuesday, November 27th

Joppin asked if I wanted to practise the chase
scene with him. I said no and changed the subject.
Joppin is practising his lines all the time. He talks
throughout the whole play and is going to have a
professional Humpty Dumpty costume from a
proper fancy dress shop. Apparently it is very
important for the narrator to look really good.

Thursday, November 29th

Today, we did a rehearsal on the school stage.
When it was the Miss Muffet bit, I had to crouch
under the box. I felt the wood creak as big Claire
sat on it. I heard everyone laugh as she ran around

73

with the spider. I saw nothing.

When it came to the green bottles rehearsal I was surprised to see Mrs Rizla carrying a huge wooden screen onto the stage. It had the words 'BOTTLE BANK' painted on it.

'Trumpet players behind there,' she said casually, pointing behind the wooden screen. 'I don't want you to upstage the bottles.'

We all obediently sat behind the screen as the bottles jumped about and fell 'into' the bottle bank at regular intervals. The whole set up meant that no one would see the trumpet players at all. I saw Mr Burple dabbing his eyes with a blue paper towel after the rehearsal.

I realized that I would not be seen once during the whole concert. I can't tell Mum and am now dreading the big day.

Friday, November 30th

Mum has bought a new camera especially for recording Joppin and me in the concert. Oh dear.

Sunday, December 9th
CONCERT EVE

Mum, Dad and the five relatives (as well as Jim Bob) were at our house, fussing around Joppin and me. They all seemed so excited. I felt sick. Everyone was chatting about their performances as children, giving me tips on how to project my voice, telling me to talk to the people at the back of the room to make sure my voice carried. I remained very quiet.

Monday, December 10th
CONCERT DAY

The concert went as expected. Joppin was brilliant. I wasn't seen.

Everyone was quiet afterwards. They were whispering congratulations to Joppin and didn't know what to say to me. Perhaps they thought they'd seen me and not recognised me? But no one mentioned it. To make matters worse I had stiff knees from crouching in that box for so long. I actually had to crouch in it for the first 30 minutes so no one would see me coming on. I then had to crawl off as inconspicuously as possible with the box still on me.

Two more performances to go but at least the one with my family watching is over. Now I can start to look forward to Christmas.

Friday, December 21st

Today was the last day of school before the Christmas holidays. It was also our last trumpet lesson of the term. Mr Stolliams said that he had presents for us, as a reward for working so hard all term.

'Go and look in my bag Maggie,' he said. 'Find the trumpet keyrings.'

His bag was large and made of leather. It was full of lots of sheets of music, loads of tissues, receipts and bits and bobs. I found the keyrings, which were really beautiful little gold trumpets.

'You're musicians now,' he said in a very serious voice. 'Work hard and be the best you can be.'

MERRY CHRISTMAS!

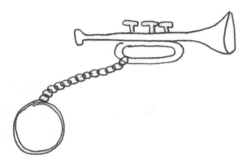

<u>Friday, January 4th</u>

Only two days until the new school term. I'm
quite looking forward to seeing everyone again;
however, there are a couple of problems relating
to my Christmas presents.

Problem 1:

Me, Holly, Mandy and Sarah agreed that we
were all going to ask for rubbers for our rubber
collections for Christmas. The plan is that we will
all take our new rubbers in on the first day back
to school to show each other. In December, when
Grandma asked me what I'd like for Christmas, I'd
said 'fancy rubbers' please.

On Christmas morning, Grandma handed me my
present. She was keenly scanning my face to see
my expression. I was so excited wondering what
shapes my rubbers would be. When I opened it I

was shocked to see that the package contained five plain white rectangular rubbers from the supermarket. NO FANCY SHAPED RUBBERS AT ALL! I tried to look delighted but inside I was crushed. I was wondering what I would show Holly, Mandy and Sarah? No doubt they will have loads of really exciting rubbers.

Problem 2:

One other problem has also emerged due to a dodgy Christmas present. Holly is having a sleepover for her birthday in four weeks' time. Much planning has gone into this; in fact we have all been planning Holly's sleepover for months. In preparation for this sleepover and others that we are planning, as well as for camping, I asked Mum and Dad for a special fold-out foam bed called a block bed. It folds up to be a chair then folds out to be a bed. My friends already have one and I'd found the perfect one on the Internet. I'd showed Dad quite a long time before Christmas so he'd have time to order it. I expected it to come folded up as the chair and be a sort of cube shape. Because of this I was mega surprised when Dad produced a really long (longer than me) cylindrical-shaped parcel from the garage. It was all wrapped in brown paper with a fancy gold bow tied round the middle.

I began to open it and saw that Mum and Dad were holding hands watching me.

'You are going to love this,' said Dad, squeezing Mum's hand.

'World's biggest sausage?' I asked. Everyone laughed and I ripped the paper off. I could see that it was shiny and pink.

'World's biggest raw sausage?' I asked. Dad was laughing. I pulled the shiny pink sausage out of the wrapper and tried to work out what it was. I could tell that it was made from an old pink sleeping bag, which had been stuffed so much that it had become the exact shape of a sausage.

'It's your new bed... for sleepovers,' said Dad.

'Do I sleep on it or in it?' I asked, trying to sound pleased while looking round hopefully for the parcel with the block bed in it.

'On it of course. It's a mattress,' Dad said, 'and you'll never believe this... I actually made it myself. I stuffed it with some of the old clothes Mum couldn't sell... clever eh?'

'Oh, thanks,' I said, desperately trying to sound like I wasn't disappointed.

Sunday, January 6th

Today is the last day of the school holidays and I have been busy trying to limit my future problems by attempting to make my Christmas presents look more acceptable.

As we are comparing our novelty rubbers tomorrow I realised that I would have to try and make my plain, white rectangular rubbers look more like fun ones.

I got my pens out and changed each rubber.

Five plain rubbers became...

A fish finger (complete with orange glitter)

A mummy in a coffin (pen drawing)

A pink finger with red fingernail

A brown parcel with string (real) and a stamp (drawn)

A bed with duvet and pillows (drawn on)

I am quite pleased with them, especially the finger that I've also trimmed slightly so it looked realistic.

I have also been lying on the sleeping sausage

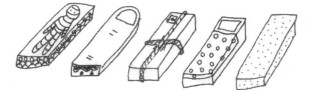

to try and flatten it a bit. I tried folding it up like the block bed but it didn't fold at all. Dad says he will put it on the roof rack to take it to Holly's sleepover. Aghaaaa!

Monday, January 7th
FIRST DAY BACK

Everyone was milling around the playground talking about Christmas presents. I kept quiet. I couldn't help but feel a little disappointed when hearing of all the fantastic gifts everyone else had got.

When we went in, we saw that Mr Burple was wearing a funny knitted jumper with a picture of reindeer on it. It even had a tiny bell sewn on under the reindeer's chin. Everyone was giggling about it saying it was babyish. I quite liked it though. The eyes of the reindeer were looking in different directions making it look confused and cute.

On the desks were sheets of paper with names on them. I found out that I would now be sitting next to Quentin. He is the biggest know-it-all in the school, and a confirmed cheat, but as long as he doesn't take his teeth out during the maths tests I can probably cope.

Mr Burple wrote on the whiteboard... DIVIDING IS SHARING.

The tiny reindeer bell tinkled as he wrote, causing much hilarity. He then handed each of us a plastic cup. Next, he emptied loads of wrapped sweets onto his desk. Everyone cheered.

'Our Christmas presents?' asked Jake.

'Our maths class,' replied Mr Burple, obviously pleased that we were taking an interest. 'Modern methods for modern teachers,' he smiled smugly.

He pointed to Quentin, Jake, Sarah and Claire. 'You four, up to the front with your cups.' They went up hopefully as Mr Burple then wrote 12 DIVIDED BY 4 on the whiteboard. He then shared out 12 sweets into the four cups.

'How many do you have each?' he asked.

Quentin, Sarah and Claire said three. Jake said one, with his mouth full.

'You must not eat them,' said Mr Burple crossly.

'It's not fair, Jake's eaten some,' cried the other children.

'He ate two so *I* need two,' shouted Claire.

Mr Burple ushered them back to their seats and wrote another sum on the board.

20 DIVIDED BY 5

He called five people up to the front. When checking the answers, he found that three more sweets had been eaten. Children who had not eaten sweets were complaining that it wasn't fair. Mr Burple looked drained.

'I'm going to go and get some plastic cubes to do this with instead,' he sighed. 'Please sit quietly for a moment.'

As he left the room, several children ran to the front and grabbed sweets, eating them greedily. Jake was throwing sweets across the classroom and children were leaping up and down to catch them. In the middle of the mayhem, Mrs Foley came in. Everyone froze.

'What is going on?' she asked sharply.

'Mr Burple brought sweets in for the maths lesson,' said Jake with his mouth full again.

Mrs Foley stormed out. We heard Mr Burple apologizing outside the room. We also heard a lot of bell tinkling. A few minutes later he came back, his jumper in a plastic bag, his face flushed. He continued the lesson using plastic bricks.

At playtime, we grabbed one of the picnic tables in the playground. Mandy, Holly and Sarah set out their new Christmas rubbers in neat rows.

Mandy
3 flowers
An ice cream sundae
A hotdog, burger and French fries set

Holly
A puppy
A cat
A kennel and a basket

Sarah
Twelve rubber skittles with a rubber ball
A nest complete with rubber eggs

All their rubbers were amazing. 'Let's see yours,' said Mandy.

'Um, oh, hold on...' I said, digging around in my pocket nervously. I was very embarrassed as I got the fish finger, the coffin, the finger, the parcel and the bed out. Everyone stared for a moment. I held my breath; hoping no one would realize they were homemade. The finger could have been bought (at a pinch) but I wasn't sure about the other ones.

'Wow,' said Holly, 'you made your own... brilliant!'

Everyone was looking at them saying how good they were.

'You're so creative,' said Sarah.

'I wish I'd got a plain one now,' said Mandy. 'I want to design my own; my parents are so mean just giving me fancy ones.'

I was amazed. My homemade rubbers were a hit. Woo A HIT!

That afternoon, I also got a good work star for my still life drawing of a twig. Things are looking good. Only five more stickers until I get a dip in the lucky bag.

Wednesday, January 17th
SAUSAGE WORRY

(None of my friends know about the sausage bed I got instead of the block bed – eek!)

Holly gave out the invitations to her birthday sleepover today. Last term, I'd talked so much about the block bed I was getting for Christmas that it had become a bit of a joke. When I got the invitation today it was addressed to 'Maggie Moore and the fold-up bed'! Oh dear. I wish I could tell them I've not got one but I just can't.... I will try and say nearer the time.

Holly's sleepover party will be on Saturday, 2nd February starting at 5.30pm and finishing the next morning at 11am. We have planned it all.

Popcorn

Games on the wii

Pizza

Movie

Midnight feast

Sleep (ho, ho, ho)

Pancakes for breakfast

Hide and seek until home time

The people going are Mandy, Sarah, Holly and me. Holly's sisters Ivy and Willow will be there too. They are older and at high school. Willow is an artist and her big paintings are displayed all around the house. Ivy plays the guitar and is actually in a band called The Red Moon Witches. I wouldn't mind being in a band, perhaps I'll ask her if they need any trumpet players. However, my main concern right now is the

SAUSAGE.

I have been lying on the sausage bed for about an hour each day to try and get it to flatten. It always looks like it is flattening but as soon as I get off it, it springs back into its plump sausage-like shape.

Another interesting thing happened today. There were posters all over school for a Weatherbrook School talent show on Saturday, March 9th. Anyone at the school can enter and the prize is £20 cash and a spot performing at a local café called Marples. The girls and I have decided we are going to do a synchronized dance. We began practising moves at playtime.

Friday, January 18th
The bed still looks like a sausage.

Quentin, Mr Burple and I had a trumpet lesson today. Trumpet is going well and I actually sound quite good (sort of). Mr Stolliams suggested that I play something in the talent show. I told him I was already doing a dance with the girls and he said that I was allowed to enter twice if one entry was with a group and one was on my own. So I signed up to play a trumpet tune, and me, Holly, Mandy and Sarah signed up to dance as a group.

Now it's just a matter of practice. I'm getting nervous, but it's five weeks to go until the show.

After school, I told Mum about my entries to the show. She was thrilled but Joppin started complaining.

'It's not fair. I want to play an instrument,' he whined. Mum explained that instrument lessons start in year three at our school but Joppin kept stomping his feet. Mum suggested that he do something else in the show. This meant that for the next hour we had to listen to him sing several songs. Joppin was so loud and insistent that Mum never asked what I was doing. It was all Joppin, Joppin, Joppin.

Saturday, January 19th

The bed still looks like a sausage.

Sunday, January 20th

The bed still looks like a sausage.

Monday, January 21st

The bed still looks like a sausage!

Friday, February 1st

You guessed it, the bed still looks like a sausage.

The sleepover at Holly's is tomorrow. No one knows about the sausage bed and I'm dreading taking it. But Dad thinks I love it so I have to take it. Eeek! Will they all laugh at me?

Sunday, February 3rd
SLEEPOVER NEWS

Dad called me outside when it was time to go to the sleepover. I was mortified to see that he had tied the huge pink sausage bed to the roof of the car. It looked ludicrous, like we were advertising sausages. I wondered if people might even stop the car to order a hot dog.

Dad said I could sit in the front. This is
something that I usually love doing as it makes me
feel grown up. But this time it just made me feel
extra embarrassed. When I got in, I could see the
tip of the sausage bobbing up and down through
the windscreen.

There were a few people on the pavement,
including some children who live on my street. I
couldn't bear being seen so I crouched down out
of sight and pretended I had something in my
shoe. I fiddled with my shoe until we got to the
next road.

Dad took the sausage car through town. I'm
sure he was choosing a long route to parade his
pink invention. He parked the car outside a

butcher's shop and gave the people coming out
the thumbs up. He laughed away at this. But I was
pinker that the sausage. Strangely, I had
something in my other shoe that needed extensive
checking.

When we got to Holly's, I hid in the car while
dad took the sausage bed inside. I didn't want to
be there the first time they saw it. Luckily, as I
had taken my shoes and socks off in the car when I
was fiddling, I made myself busy putting them
back on again, slowly. This was an excellent
excuse to stay in the car for a bit longer.

I watched Dad as he bundled the sausage
through Holly's front door. I then heard howls of
laughter coming from inside. Through the window
I could see the sausage bed being carried about.

I had to be brave. It would look odd if I was in
the car for too long. I took a deep breath and
tried to shut the worry out of my brain. I jumped
out of the car and ran inside the house. Holly,
Mandy and Sarah were all lying over the sausage
bed rocking back and forth.

'Great giant worm,' said Mandy as they all
rolled forward and walked with their hands until

just their feet were on it. It looked quite fun so I joined in. Dad offered to take the sausage bed upstairs but everyone wanted to play with it. He gave me a big kiss then left. I gave Holly her present and she said she would open it later.

The first thing we had planned to do was play games on the wii. But everyone wanted to play worm games with the sausage (worm) bed.

Worm games played at the party:

Hide the worm (quite funny because the worm was always obviously visible)

Trampolining while riding a worm (on Holly's garden trampoline).

Balancing on the worm while everyone tried to roll you off

Running along the worm's back without slipping off (impossible)

Rolling about under the worm pretending to be the victim of a giant worm attack

We were playing the 'roll under the worm' game, when Holly's sisters, Ivy and Willow, suggested making a worm horror film. We all loved the idea so after tea, Ivy got her phone out and began filming us. We all crept about pretending to be scared then took it in turns to be attacked by the giant worm. It was really funny.

After we'd made the film, Holly opened her presents. She got...

From Mandy – a money box with digital display that tells you how much you have put in (quite good).

From Sarah – a remote control spider.

From Me – a nail art kit.

After the presents, we went upstairs. My sausage bed (now known as 'the worm') was outside on the trampoline. I looked at it out of the window. It had seemed so full of life earlier but now it just lay still, as if all the excitement had killed it. I was just figuring out how to get it upstairs ready for bedtime when Holly called me to the bathroom.

'I didn't want to say in front of the others,' she whispered, 'but the giant worm is my best present, thank you.'

I looked at her, my mouth dropped open. She thought my sausage bed was a present?! A big giant worm birthday present! I quickly changed my shocked mouth for an emergency smile.

'Great,' I said, my heart beating really fast, my brain wondering where I'd sleep and what I'd say to Dad.

Holly's dad thought I'd simply forgotten my bed so he got a spare blow-up one out of the garage. We stayed up late and watched the worm horror film loads of times and ate popcorn. We were up so late that Holly's mum had to come in and tell us off. Eventually we all settled down in our beds, I was really comfy snuggled in a big orange blanket that Holly's mum had lent me; it was a relief not to be balanced on the sausage (worm). I lay awake for a while staring into the unfamiliar darkness, wondering what I'd say to Dad when he came to collect the sausage and me in the morning.

Next day, we all sat at the old wooden kitchen table. Holly's mum had made a pile of pancakes and had put lots of toppings out.

Pancake toppings:

Lemon juice

Sugar

Jam

Syrup

Cornflakes

Chocolate spread

Peanut butter

Bananas

Holly wrapped her pancake around cornflakes. She crunched it, smiling enthusiastically, but I don't think it could have tasted that great. I had banana and jam, which was yumalicious.

After breakfast, we watched telly as we waited for our parents to arrive. I was pretty worried and watched out of the window, getting ready to run out and speak to Dad before he got out of the car. He had to know that we couldn't take the sausage home.

When he arrived, I leapt off the sofa and ran out. I told him everything, all about the misunderstanding. I thought he'd be annoyed but he started laughing.

'Promise you won't say anything,' I begged.

'OK darling,' he said.

We said goodbye to everyone and left. Dad was laughing and making fun of me all the way home, but I was mega relieved that Holly didn't find out the truth.

Friday, February 8th

Holly said she loved the worm so much she'd tried to sleep on it last night. However, because of the silky cover, she'd slipped off just before midnight and ended up sleeping on the floor.

There's only four weeks to go until the talent show and we've decided to practise the dance every playtime. We've nearly got all the moves sorted out and it's starting to look pretty good. As for trumpet, I am practising this tune called 'Eye Of The Tiger' every day and can nearly play if off by heart. Joppin is going to do a strange dance where he pretends to be a bubble.

Monday, February 11th

We just found out today that a new boy is joining our class next week. I wonder what he will be like.

Wednesday, February 13th

I found one of Joppin's old socks stuffed in the end of my trumpet. Gross.

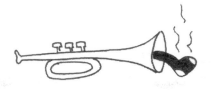

Monday, February 18th

When we arrived at school today, the word
'Rush' was written on the whiteboard. So we all
rushed to our seats, as quickly as we could,
wondering what was going on and why we had to
rush. We sat and waited. Mr Burple opened the
door followed by a small blond boy with bright
blue eyes and scruffy hair.

'This is Rush Seymour,' Mr Burple said, patting
the boy on the head awkwardly.

'Hi,' the boy said shyly, looking down.

Mr Burple directed him to an empty desk and
he sat down.

'Jake, you will chum Rush at playtime,
introduce him to a few people,' said Mr Burple as
he cleared the whiteboard and wrote 'MaThs is
FUn' on it instead. Jake nodded.

Mr Burple then got out 50 plastic apples, some
eye masks and some swag bags.

'It's all about taking away.' He put on a television game show voice and said... 'Who wants to be a... robber of apples?' He waved two apples above his head excitedly. No one volunteered. In fact the classroom went very quiet.

'No one would want to steal a plastic apple,' said Jake eventually.

'It doesn't matter,' Mr Burple said, loosing enthusiasm. 'It's the fun of the game that's important.'

In the end, no one volunteered so Mr Burple was the robber. He sneaked around putting plastic apples in his bag while everyone watched in silence. It went on for a bit too long.

At playtime, everyone crowded round Jake and Rush. People were bombarding him with questions.

Questions Rush was asked:

What football team do you support?

Have you just moved house?

Where do you live?

What was your old school called and what was it like?

What do you think of Mr Burple?

Rush told us that he was expelled from his previous school for breaking a window and repeatedly wrestling in the toilets! Apparently the kids were scared at him because he was so good at pinning people down on the floor. One sadder thing he said was that his dad has been in prison for years and he never sees him. He told us in great detail about the raid on his house where his dad was bundled into a police car and taken away. It sounded terrible.

I feel sorry for Rush, but I'm also a bit worried about having a naughty boy in our class. Jake is bad enough.

After playtime, we did History; our new topic is Victorian times. It was actually quite interesting as it was all about Victorian inventions. Some were really useful like photography, cars and telephones but there were lots of weird ones like peddle swimming machines, a flying machine that was attached to birds and a hat with a pop-up umbrella. Mr Burple put some pictures of original drawings on the whiteboard. It made me realise why people would want to be inventors, it would be fun making up really bizarre inventions.

Perhaps I'll invent something; I could always go into Dad's shed for bits.

After lunch, Mr Burple told us that we were going on a trip a week on Friday to a Victorian inventions exhibition at the town museum. He gave us each a permission letter to take home. The letter also asked if any parents could help. I haven't shown Dad the letter yet, but I really hope he doesn't want to come. He'd be hours in there, looking at everything in great detail. He'd forget he was meant to be there for the children.

Tuesday, February 19th

After school today, I gave Dad the letter about the trip. Luckily he couldn't make it as a helper. He is inventing an inside/outside machine with Jim Bob that day. I'm not sure what an inside/outside machine is but I hope it doesn't end up in my bedroom.

I also practised my trumpet. It's starting to sound pretty good.

Friday, February 22nd

Rush seems to be settling in well and I haven't heard of any wrestling or pinning down going on. He did lock himself in the toilet for 20 minutes, but he was on his own. He said he needed to 'take his time with these matters'.

Another strange thing I found out today is that

Rush plays the trumpet. He joined the trumpet class with me, Quentin and Mr Burple. He has this strange trumpet that he brought with him. The end of it was all crumpled up and he introduced it as 'the crumpet'. He says it is a family treasure so he can't ever change it. It looks really funny, like he's walked into a wall while playing it. He says he's been playing for years, but it doesn't sound like it. He sometimes plays the right notes, but he often just plays randomly.

It's hard for Mr Stolliams because he wants to start Rush off at the beginning of the beginner book, but Rush keeps talking about how brilliant he is. He even said that he doesn't need to look at the notes because he can 'feel the music'.

Quentin freaked him out with his teeth though. When Rush saw them, glistening on his knee, he leapt in the air screaming, his arms flying about in horror.

I got a good work sticker for my drawing of

Queen Victoria. I now only have four stars to go.

Monday, February 25th
Sarah got a dip in the bag today. She got an amazing rainbow pencil that draws rainbow-coloured lines. We all had a go with it.

Friday, March 1st
VICTORIAN TRIP

We had the Victorian trip today and something very interesting happened. We were in the classroom, getting ready to go when four parent helpers came in. Holly's mum, Claire's mum, Quentin's dad, (who's a chef and was wearing an apron – strange), and another man I didn't recognize.

Mr Burple introduced the unknown man as Mr Seymour, Rush's dad! Everyone went quiet. Rush's dad was meant to be in prison, Rush hadn't seen him for years. We all started mumbling. I was worried that he may be a dangerous criminal and I wondered if Mr Burple knew. I wondered if it would be safe on the bus. Rush looked at his desk, avoiding eye contact.

On the bus, Rush sat next to his dad. Jake and Peter sat in front of them with Holly and me just across the aisle. We were listening in to see if we could hear anything interesting.

'When did you get out?' Jake asked Rush's dad from between the seats in front.

'Out of the house?' asked Mr Seymour, confused.

Rush jumped in... 'Oh, um last week wasn't it, now let's play a game. Let's play eye spy. Eye spy something beginning with 'R',' he said urgently.

'What were you in for?' Jake asked Mr Seymour.

'Um, breakfast?' he answered.

'Can anyone guess?' said Rush, 'what begins with 'R'? It could be rabbit but it's not.'

'We know about you being in jail,' said Peter matter-of-factly.

'No one guessing? It's 'road',' said Rush... 'Another go?'

Rush's dad looked at Rush. Rush went quiet.

'I have never been in jail. The mere thought of it! I'm a very respectable man.'

Rush went bright red.

'Something beginning with 'S'?' he said hopefully.

'Was Rush expelled from his last school?' asked Jake.

'Of course not,' said Mr Seymour. 'Rush moved school because the kids were too rough for him. Rush is a big softy.'

Rush frantically rubbed steam off the window. His hands were shaking.

Jake and Peter were giggling and muttering to each other. Rush's dad looked cross and Rush looked out of the window not wanting to face anyone.

''S' was for sky,' Rush said quietly to himself, still facing the window.

'We will have a talk later,' said his dad.

Holly and I looked at each other, our eyebrows raised. I was relieved there wasn't a dangerous criminal on the bus.

AT THE MUSEUM

We rushed into the museum. The exhibition was quite good. They had a Victorian camera where you could stand under a sheet. We all had a go. They had a really old car, a weird pedal shower bath where you sit on a stool in a bath, peddling to make the water come out. We weren't allowed to try that one. They had various other strange contraptions. There were also photos and drawings on the wall.

We were all looking round when a strange-looking woman joined our group. She wore a long corduroy skirt and a strange white shirt with lots of ruffles around the neck. Her face was covered in thick white powder. There was even white powder on her lips, which made her look really strange. Her very pale hair was pulled up in a tight bun on her head. We wondered if she was dressed up as a Victorian but Holly said she was definitely either a Victorian ghost or a lady dressed up as a Victorian ghost. It began to creep me out a bit that a ghost may be following us around. But we suspected she was part of the exhibition.

'Go and touch her and see if she's solid or vapour,' whispered Holly.

I crept over and stood behind her. I reached out slowly and touched her on the arm. It was solid and I was very startled when she spun round and said 'Hello'.

'Oh hi,' I said, 'good exhibition.'

'Isn't it wonderful, don't you wish you'd been born a hundred and fifty years ago?' she said in a warbling, high voice.

'Not sure,' I replied, 'that would mean I wouldn't be here now.'

The woman began laughing, saying how funny I was. She kind of joined our group after that. We felt a bit guilty because she was probably meant to be showing everyone around the museum, but she was mainly looking at things with us, telling us all sorts of interesting things about the inventions.

'What's your name?' asked Holly.

'Bethalina,' said the lady.

After the trip we were rather surprised when the lady got on the bus with us. Everyone began talking about it, thinking the woman had made a mistake. She sat down next to Mr Burple, who was just in front of Holly and me.

'Are you coming with us?' Peter asked Bethalina.

'Of course,' she replied.

'Don't you need to stay at the museum?' asked Holly.

'No, why would I?'

'Well you're sort of, part of the exhibition,' Holly said.

Mr Burple went purple and cross.

'How dare you!' he said. Holly wilted in her seat.

'That's very rude,' said Bethalina more calmly.

We were gobsmacked.

'This lady,' said Mr Burple, 'is Bethalina Burple, my wife!'

'Oh sorry,' mumbled Holly.

We were surprised, but it did explain the knee patches sewn onto her long cord skirt. Looking again we could see that she matched Mr Burple perfectly. I wasn't sure the white powder on the face was the best look, but each to their own.

Monday, March 4th

Rush has gone very quiet at school now. He just sits looking rather embarrassed.

The talent show date is approaching fast. The synchronised dance is looking good. The trumpet is sounding good. I'm nervous and my tummy feels like jelly when I think about it, but I'm sort of looking forward to it now.

Joppin has been practising his act too. He is going to go on dressed up as a bubble. He will then do what he calls his 'bubble dance'. After that he will get some bubble liquid out of his sleeve and blow some real bubbles. He is convinced he is going to win, but I'm not so sure. Let's just say his bubble outfit looks more like a clear plastic bag hanging over his shoulders, and you can see his white pants through it. He says everyone finds pants very funny so he will definitely win.

Friday, March 8th

The talent show is tomorrow, everyone came to my house for a quick last practice, and it went quite well. I had a trumpet practice too and I think I'm ready.

Saturday, March 9th
TALENT SHOW!

Oh my gosh, the talent show was today. I can hardly believe all the things that happened.

Because the school hall is quite small, the talent show was held in a local theatre. It was really busy. Every seat was full. Performers got to sit in the front three rows ready to be called up. Parents and non-performing kids sat in the other seats. At the side of the stage there was a table where the two judges were sitting. The judges were...

Mrs Marple – she owns a local café that runs all sorts of events. Part of the talent show prize is to be given a chance to perform at the cafe, Marples.

Dave Tanner – He is a local radio DJ. He was wearing a t-shirt with his own name on it. He is well known for being a bit silly.

The running list was stuck on the wall. The group dance was quite early on, but me playing the trumpet was the very last act. There were twenty-eight acts all together. I will write down information on the most relevant ones.

Details of performances

Joppin

Joppin was first on. The theatre was full and everyone was waiting. Mrs Marple and Dave Tanner had their pencils and notebooks ready. Joppin walked on. He suddenly looked very tiny up there. His plastic bag was hanging off his little shoulders. He danced and jumped. Then he tried to blow some bubbles but none came out. He got out the bubble liquid tube and tipped it upside down. It was empty. Everyone clapped kindly but I saw Mrs Marple and Dave Tanner look at each other and shake their heads.

Peter

Peter was on straight after Joppin. He was going to tell a joke. He walked on and immediately slipped over; he landed with a loud thud on his bottom. No one knew if that was the act or not so a few people clapped. Mr Burple had to come on with a mop, to mop up spilled bubble liquid. Eventually Peter got up.

'What do you call a man with a spade on his head?' Peter said.

'Doug,' shouted the audience.

Peter shuffled off.

Me, Holly, Sarah and Mandy (dancing)

The music started and my heart was beating like mad. We stood in a row and started our dance. It was going quite well. Then I noticed that Sarah was doing everything back to front. After our performance we ran off asking what happened. Sarah began crying saying that she'd practised in front of the mirror so much last night that she couldn't remember what was real life and what was mirror life.

Quentin

Quentin went on dressed in a suit and top hat. First he made his teeth disappear. This involved him holding his false teeth behind his back and doing a big gummy smile. Everyone cheered, amazed. He then called for a volunteer.

Mr Burple went up and Quentin asked him for his wedding ring. Mr Burple handed it over and Quentin made it disappear. Only problem was that he couldn't make it reappear. After looking everywhere, with Mr Burple, Quentin and various others crawling around the floor, it was decided that the show should carry on anyway. Mr Burple stood glaring at Quentin.

Various other acts

Nothing much to report on the other acts, bit of singing, bit of comedy, bit of music playing... bit boring.

My trumpet act

I walked on with my trumpet. I stood facing the judges and side on to the audience. I began playing 'Eye Of The Tiger'. Horrifyingly, it sounded very quiet. I wasn't sure if it was nerves or if there was something in my trumpet. I carried on, blowing as hard as I could. The tune could only just be heard. I was so upset I nearly cried.

Suddenly a pair of Joppin's yellow and green underpants shot out of the end of the trumpet. They flew across the stage and landed on Mrs Marples's head.

I carried on, now at full volume, and finished the song. Mrs Marple and Dave Tanner were in hysterics about the flying pants and, when I finished playing, everyone stood up to cheer.

Dave Tanner walked over to me.

'I think we have our winner,' he said, beaming at me. 'The pant-shooting trumpet player wins.' He took my trumpet and held it high in the air as the audience cheered and whooped. 'I can't wait to see more pant flying action at Marples.'

'And I just loved those frumpy old-fashioned underpants,' laughed Mrs Marple.

I was so happy. My first ever win. It felt amazing. Mum and Dad, who'd been in the audience, were so proud of me. All the way home they were saying how brilliant it had been. Joppin wouldn't talk to me.

Monday, March 11th

Everyone is talking about how funny my act was. They were asking how I got the pants to shoot out at just the right moment. I will be getting the money part of my prize in assembly on Friday: £20 and a spot performing at Marples! My concern now is that everyone will want me to shoot yellow and green underpants out of my trumpet at Marples and I'm not sure if I can do it again. I will have to start practising. I will have to raid Joppin's pant drawer later. Luckily the gig isn't until May 21st so I have more than two months to perfect the act.

Friday, March 15th

Mr Stolliams hadn't seen the talent show but he'd heard that I'd won. He was so pleased and said what a great teacher he was.

'I'm so glad a serious musician won,' he said. 'So much better than some silly novelty act winning.'

Quentin and Rush giggled, but no one told Mr Stolliams about the underpants.

'I will definitely come to the Marples gig,' he said. 'It will be marvellous to see you perform there.'

Oh no!

Saturday, March 16th

Joppin has agreed to let me borrow his underpants so long as he can help with the Marples act. I agreed, as I am nervous about doing it on my own. He thought that more things coming out of the trumpet was the way to go. He poured some bubble liquid in and we got three bubbles out. I haven't managed to shoot the pants out again yet, which is a worry. I am also looking for some serious music to play (to satisfy Mr Stolliams).

Monday, March 18th

My mind keeps thinking about the Marples gig and what might go wrong. Today, we started a new project at school. This is good news as it is giving me something else to think about.

GARDENING PROJECT

We are all going to be gardeners. Everyone in the class has been given a small plot of land in this soil area near the playground. It has been sectioned off into squares (with string). We each have our own square. We made name posts today. We all got a piece of wood that looked like a big lolly stick and had to paint our name on it with enamel paint and stick it in our square. Mr Burple is going to get loads of seeds and we can choose what we want to grow.

Wednesday, March 20th

I've been practising for Marples (even though there's quite a while to go). I don't know how I got those underpants to fly out at the talent show. I haven't been able to do it again.

Tuesday, March 26th

We all started planting seeds this week. We are allowed to add seeds to our plots whenever we want. I am growing sunflowers, strawberries and red poppies. Quentin is only growing aubergines and has planted about forty seeds. This seems very odd. Does anyone actually eat aubergines?

Peter says that he is only going to grow one small flower right in the middle of his plot. He spent ages raking the soil, and then he made a small hole in the middle with his finger. He then carefully put just one seed in the middle. He said that this is going to be a minimalist garden and that he may add one pebble later to go with the flower.

When Peter went in to get a drink, Quentin leapt up and ran to Peter's square. He then sprinkled loads of seeds all over the plot while laughing.

'Not going to be quite so minimalist now,' he said to Jake as he emptied another handful of seeds onto the soil. He did a quick rake over so Peter wouldn't notice.

'What's the opposite of minimalist?' Quentin asked. No one answered.

Wednesday, March 27th

I can't believe it's the Easter holidays next week. Mr Burple has been doing Easter-themed lessons for everything. Egg box maths, chick art, bunny literacy... you name it, he's made it Eastery.

Sarah is having her birthday party on Friday. It is an 'art' party. This local artist has opened up her studio for parties. Apparently, we're going to do a piece of art in the studio then go back to Sarah's house for a party tea. I'm quite looking forward to it, as I'm good at art. I'm really good at detail, like drawing the stitches on clothes, or doing loads of leaves on a tree.

Holly is dreading it because she can only draw one thing: a strange cat with eyes like purple spirals. Whenever we have to do a picture in art she draws the cat. No one knows where the idea came from. Holly thinks it was something to do with a past life.

Sarah's dad is really into computers and he has this website where he writes a blog about parenting. It's always really embarrassing for Sarah because he writes loads of stuff about her and takes photos. There was this time when Sarah forgot to learn her spellings and only got two out of ten. Her dad wrote a whole piece about it and even took a photo of the test and added that to the page. I'm quite glad my dad bumbles around in his workshop sawing bits of wood. (In a way.)

Sarah's dad wants to take photos of the art party to put on his blog. At the bottom of the invitations there was a form for our parents to sign asking if he could use photos of us on his website. Mum wrote on my form 'only if Maggie agrees and likes them'. This was quite a relief, as I'd hate it if there were terrible photos of me floating around online for years.

Thursday, March 28th

Good news! I managed to get seven bubbles to come out of the trumpet today. Things are looking good for the Marples show.

Sarah's party is tomorrow. My mum bought a birthday present for her and wrapped it up ready for me to take to the party. It's a bit embarrassing as it's a maths book called 'Miranda Mouse Minute Maths'. I told Mum it was totally unsuitable for a birthday gift but she says it's too late to get anything else now. I am dreading Sarah opening it and it is currently overshadowing the whole event for me.

Friday, March 29th
Sarah's Birthday Party - update

The invitation said 'Plantana Cottage Studio' so I was expecting a nice cottage in the countryside. When Dad pulled up at the address I was surprised to see it was in a large block of flats. We waited for the lift. It was all smelly and graffiti was written all the walls. Dad was going to leave me at the party but suddenly decided to stay.

We went up to the eighteenth floor. There was a sign on the door saying 'Plantana Cottage – dream it, believe it, achieve it'. We knocked on the door and Sarah's dad let us in. The inside of the flat was quite unusual. All the walls were painted yellow and there were lots of shelves. On the shelves were loads of teapots, they were all different shapes and colours. In each teapot was a different type of cactus or succulent plant. They actually looked really good.

Sarah, Holly and Mandy called me through to the art room, which was the room that would have been the lounge. It had a big table in the middle and shelves full of art materials around the side. There were cactus teapots on the top shelves and above them hung several large paintings. The paintings looked like smudges of different coloured paint swirled together.

'Sit down, sit down,' said Holly, patting the stool next to her, 'Sandra Beer-Horn, the artist, is just getting drinks.'

I sat down, dying to know what Sandra Beer-Horn would be like. Dad started chatting to Sarah's dad who was already taking photos.

Suddenly Sandra Beer-Horn walked in carrying a tray with a jug of juice and lots of teacups in different colours.

Sandra was a weathered lady with a lopsided grin and long white hair. She wore orange dungarees over a navy blue polo neck jumper. In the front of her dungarees was a large pocket full of paintbrushes, pens and spanners. She sat with us and poured out the juice.

'Paint or draw something that tells me who you are,' she said, handing out the dr⋯ s. 'Whoever I feel expresses themselves ⋯ ., can choose a cactus teapot to take home.'

I very much wanted to take home a cactus teapot, as they looked amazing. I particularly liked one that was in a rainbow-striped pot with a funny crooked cactus poking out at a funny angle.

We drank juice and began drawing and painting. Sarah, trying to copy the paintings on the wall I think, got lots of bright paints out and began swirling them around. I decided to be true to myself and began a detailed self-portrait in pencil. I drew myself carefully, making sure to put all the detail in, lots of pockets, stitching and even belt holes. After I'd done it, I went over all the pencil in black pen to make it stand out more.

Holly drew a massive cat with purple spiral eyes. She painted it with different-coloured patches then drew coloured lines radiating out of it. Mandy drew all her favourite belongings including her game console, TV, handbag, rubber collection, and phone.

Sandra Beer-Horn was giving the two dads a tour of the flat while we got on with the art. She was showing Sarah's dad all her paintings and asking if he wanted to put any on his website.

I was pretty hopeful that the teapot would be mine as my picture looked really professional. I just needed a blue felt tip to do the eyes. I thought it would look a bit mysterious if the only colour in the picture was a tiny bit of blue on the eyes. I leant over to get the pen when suddenly I knocked a paint pot full of red paint all over my picture. Only the head, one arm, one shoulder and one foot could be seen. I yelled in alarm but nothing could be done and there wasn't time to redo it.

Suddenly Sandra and the two dads came back in. Sarah's dad began taking pictures of our artwork and us. He even got a shot of my totally ruined picture. Sandra came up behind me and looked over my shoulder.

'I know,' I said sadly.

'I love this,' she said, 'we cover part of our beings with unauthentic conformity, is that what the red represents?'

'Oh, um yes,' I mumbled, confused.

Sarah's dad had been listening to what Sandra was saying. 'You mean red is the hidden part of who we are?' he asked.

'Yes,' said Sandra. 'It's what we hide behind in life.'

I didn't know what they were talking about but Sandra and the two dads talked about my painting for quite a while and amazingly, I won the teapot!

Back at Sarah's...

After that, we all went back to Sarah's house for tea. We played with Sarah's baby sister, Bobo, for a while then had a very nice party tea with sausage rolls and pink wafer biscuits. After the tea came the moment I was dreading. Present opening time. (Miranda Mouse – eeeeeek). There was fifteen minutes left until the end of the party. I figured that if I could delay the opening of the presents somehow then she would open them later, after we'd gone home, and that would be far less embarrassing.

'Let's play tig,' I shouted.

'Maybe after the presents,' said Sarah.

'Um, did you hear that?' I said.

'No, what?' said Holly.

'I think someone's at the door.'

'Dad will get it, now presents.' Sarah held her first present. Luckily it wasn't Miranda Mouse Minute Maths. She opened it. It was a design your own t-shirt kit from Mandy.

'It's from America,' said Mandy proudly.

It was really good. It came with fabric paints, sequins, buttons and a plain white t-shirt to design onto.

'I absolutely love it,' said Sarah, she went over and gave Mandy a big hug. I eyed the clock, twelve minutes to go. She got the next present. Luckily it wasn't Miranda Mouse Minute Maths. It was from Holly. She opened it. It was a really fantastic bag. It looked like it was made from a pair of jeans and even had a real belt around the top.

'Oh it's great.' Sarah said, squealing with excitement. She put it over her shoulder and walked around. Then she gave Holly a big hug.

There was just one present left. I looked at the clock, seven minutes to go.

'Aghh, a spider!' I said, jumping up. 'It went

that way,' I said and pointed at Sarah's bed.

'Dad will get it,' Sarah said, picking up the last present. I felt hot and sweaty as she unwrapped it. She pulled the book out.

'Miranda Mouse Minute Maths?' she said holding it up. Everyone laughed and I went red. 'You are funny Maggie. My dad does that too, he always gets me a joke present. This year he got me a toenail clipping box with a real toenail clipping in it.' I tried to smile, aware that I didn't get a hug.

We spent the last few minutes of the party looking at this world records book that Sarah had got from her dad. There were some amazing records like…

*Longest distance to spit a watermelon seed –
21 metres*

Fastest talker – 260 words in 23 seconds

*Most spoons balanced on face – 15 for 30
seconds*

Longest maggot bath – 90 minutes

*Longest time to stand on a gym ball – 5 hours
and 7 minutes*

'Let's break a world record,' said Sarah. We all agreed, but what record could we break? Sarah said she'd bring the book in after the holidays for ideas.

I brought the teapot home and it now lives on my windowsill and looks brilliant.

Saturday, April 6th

Just got back from four terrible days of camping. There was snow on the roof of the tent making it cave inwards. I was freezing in the night. The one and only good thing about camping is that I now appreciate being home in my proper bed. That first night back I didn't even mind that my duvet cover was made from an old tablecloth.

Sunday, April 7th

I told Mum about the world records, including the one about the longest time to stand on a gym ball. It turns out she's got an old gym ball that she used to lie on before I was born. She got it out for me to have a go on. It was bigger than I expected, nearly coming up to my waist. I managed to stand on it for ages. It's quite floppy as it's been in the garage for years. Dad said it needed pumping up a bit with a bike pump but he couldn't find one. Still, if I can stand on it when it's floppy then imagine how good I'll be when it's really solid.

I stood on it for at least 30 minutes. With a bit of practice I reckon I could smash the world record.

Monday, April 15th

Today was the first day back at school after the holidays. Mandy has been to America for Easter and was showing us her new things from the stationery shop.

Mandy's new items:

A bendy ruler called a 'flexi curve'

A rabbit rubber with movable arms and legs

Ten fragranced gel pens, each pen has a different smell

Really amazing t-shirt with a monkey picture on it

Gold glitter nail polish

All I have from my holiday is a nasty scratch across my leg. Mum made us go on a long, cold walk. I had to climb over a wall with barbed wire on the other side. I was so cold that I didn't notice the scratch until we got back to the tent.

Tuesday, April 16th

Mandy got her tenth good work star and had a dip in the lucky bag. She got a pair of rubbers shaped like trainers. She put her fingers in each one and walked them around the table.

'Yippee, another one for my rubber collection,' she said, jumping her fingers up in the air.

I only have six good work stickers. Most people have had a dip in the lucky bag now but Mr Burple doesn't seem to notice my good work. I looked at my sticker chart on the wall. The girl in the self-portrait looks so keen and eager, a bit different from the disappointed girl I am now. Things could be worse I suppose; at least I'm not camping in the snow.

Wednesday, April 17th

At playtime we looked in Sarah's world records book. Sarah wanted to try breaking the spitting a watermelon seed record and, as she had an orange for her snack, decided to have a go with the orange seed. She wanted to see if her seed spit was near the 21-metre record so got it ready and then spat it out, it flew out about 10cm then landed on her foot. Oh dear.

Holly wanted to do the longest amount of time lying in a maggot bath. The current record is 1 hour and 30 minutes. She said she could easily lie in the bath for that long. I told her that the bath had to be full of live maggots. She decided against it.

I then told them about my mum's gym ball. The record for the longest time standing on a gym ball is five hours and seven minutes. I told them that I had stood on Mum's gym ball for ages, no problem. They all got very excited and it was decided that the gym ball standing record was the one to break. I'd better start practising.

Saturday, April 20th

I stood on the gym ball for 38 minutes today. I could have stayed on longer but tea was ready.

Monday, April 22nd

I had a funny Maths lesson today. Mr Burple wrote **'EVERYONE IS A NUMBER'** on the whiteboard in big letters. Then everybody was given a number to be between 1 and 12. (I was 6.) He then called out numbers and if the number called out was in your times table, you had to jump up and shout 'Multiple of me'.

When he called out thirty, me (6), Jake (5), Mandy (10), Quentin (3) and Claire (1) all jumped up. There were lots more goes with different numbers. It wasn't really fair because some people were jumping up a lot more than others. Claire (1) jumped up every time.

It was quite fun but Peter Potter spoiled it by crying. He kept saying, 'I'm not a number, I'm a real boy.'

Mr Burple looked a bit worried and shut the classroom door in case Mrs Foley walked past.

Tuesday, April 23rd
I stood on the gym ball for 57 minutes today.

Friday, April 26th
HAD TRUMPET LESSON TODAY

Rush spoiled trumpet lesson today. In the middle of us all playing a song, he stood up. He then proceeded to walk across the room and banged into the wall, trumpet first. He looked at his (already) crumpled trumpet and said 'Oh no, my crumpet'. We tried to carry on playing but it was very annoying.

At the end of the lesson Mr Stolliams took me to one side and said he'd give me extra lessons ready for my performance at Marples. I had to stay behind and look through some sheet music. In the end I decided on 'My Heart Will Go On', which is the theme tune to the film, 'Titanic'.

When I told Joppin about the song choice, he was disappointed at first. He then had the idea of dressing up as a heart with a headband, knee socks and trainers, and running on the spot next to me for the whole song. I'm not sure what Mr Stolliams is going to make of it but I guess it could be funny. We had a practice and even got six bubbles to come out of the trumpet. We also managed to get Joppin's underpants to come out. They didn't fly out though. They kind of hung out of the end of the trumpet and then fell when I shook it a bit.

Saturday, April 27th

I stood on the gym ball for 65 minutes today. I really think I'd be able to stand on it all day. It is so easy.

Sarah told her dad about the world record attempt and he's written about it in his blog!

Monday, April 29th

Apparently the record attempt is attracting lots of interest online. People want to know when it is happening. Sarah's dad rang my dad who confirmed that I'd been practising and was keen to do it. They then rang the school and … on Saturday, June 22nd at 10 am, I am doing my record attempt. It is taking place in the school hall!

Tuesday, April 30th

Things are going from strange to scary. An official from the world record company is coming along on June 22nd to oversee the record attempt.

Blimey, I can't believe it! It will be amazing to have my name in the book. Perhaps they will even include a picture of me standing on the ball.

Wednesday, May 1st
PLANTING PROJECT

I planted some more seeds today in my planting area. A few shoots are coming up, but all the plots looks a bit rubbish.

Peter has quite a lot of shoots coming up but he keeps pulling them out complaining about weeds.

Holly got a dip in the lucky bag and got an amazing secret spy pen. You write with invisible ink, and then a light on the other end of the pen reveals what you have written.

I stood on the gym ball for 1 hour and 17 minutes. I'm getting a bit fed up with doing it now. I really don't think I need to practise any more as I know I can stand on it for as long as I like. I will just have to make sure I'm not going to need a wee on the day.

Thursday, May 2nd

I practised trumpet today. It is starting to
sound quite good. Joppin is getting his heart outfit
ready. Mum is sewing it for him. She said how
lovely it is to see us doing things together. The gig
is in three weeks.

Friday, May 3rd

I am starting to get even more worried about
the Marples gig. Mr Stolliams keeps telling me I'm
a proper, serious musician now and how he can't
wait to see me perform. He doesn't know that
Joppin is going to be jumping around dressed as a
heart as I blow bubbles and pants out of the
trumpet. I wonder if I could find a way to stop Mr
Stolliams going to the gig.

Monday, May 6th

The Marples gig is in 13 days and we have been
thinking of ways to distract Mr Stolliams so that he
doesn't see any of the silly parts of the act.

We all sat around at the lunchtime play and wrote down possible ways to stop him seeing pants.

Ideas

Holly stands in front of him or accidentally places a bucket (or similar) over his head.

We pretend the police are outside and need to speak to him. (Sarah could perhaps dress up as a policewoman?)

Somebody holds a 'Go Maggie' banner up, obstructing his view.

We tell him the gig is cancelled due to illness.

We tell him that an unknown naughty person has been leaving pants around. (This would make it look like the naughty person just happened to leave the pants in my trumpet.)

We decided on the last idea. (The unknown naughty person option.) In fact we decided that if pants were found all over the place, pants flying out of a trumpet wouldn't seem strange at all. It would almost seem normal for pants to be in a trumpet. Mr Stolliams would just think that the naughty pant leaver was at it again and he would never suspect me.

After school I gave Mandy my £20 prize money. She lives next to a supermarket that sells pants. She popped in and bought 16 pairs of underpants. Now for the important work of deciding where to put them.

Friday, May 10th
OPERATION UNDERPANTS PART 1

I sneaked into the music room before anyone arrived and put a pair of underpants in the end of each trumpet. I also put a pair hanging from the light and a pair hanging off the whiteboard.

When the trumpet lesson started, everyone was blowing away unsuccessfully. Then, one by one, each person pulled a pair of underpants out of the end of their trumpet.

'This is very strange,' said Mr Burple, holding his pair up.

'Oh yeah, underpants keep appearing all over the place,' I said. 'I must have seen 30 pairs this week.'

Quentin and Rush looked at me suspiciously.

'It's a disgrace,' said Mr Stolliams, putting all the pants in the bin. 'It's very unpleasant and not at all funny. At least we know we're all sensible in this class.'

Friday, May 17th
OPERATION UNDERPANTS PART 2

During today's trumpet lesson, Holly threw underpants through the music room window. They landed on Quentin's knee, on top of the teeth. 'Eeeeeuuuuuuuw, pants on my teeth,' he shrieked. 'I've got to wash my teeth.' He rushed off to the toilet. Mr Stolliams sighed deeply and put the pants into the bin.

'Blimey, I hope no one puts underpants in my trumpet at Marples,' I said.

At the end of the lesson, Mr Stolliams stood up. 'It is a disgrace that these pants are distracting us from our important musical learning,' he said pacing around, 'I've got a good mind to call the police if this carries on.' We all nodded. Oh dear, looks like operation underpants didn't work. We are going to have to resort to idea number one.

Idea 1 – Holly stands in front of Mr Stolliams or accidentally places a bucket (or similar) over his head.

Sunday, May 19th
THE MARPLES GIG

Well it has all happened. The show at Marples was today. It was packed. Loads of teachers, parents, kids and random members of the public were there. Mr Stolliams sat in the second row. He was just in front of Sarah, baby Bobo and Mandy. Holly sat in front of him (all carefully planned). My

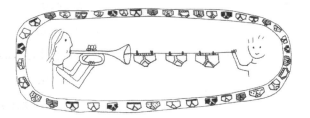

mum and dad were right at the front filming the whole thing.

Joppin had this brilliant idea of pulling a washing line full of underpants out of the trumpet at the beginning. As he did it, Holly stood up, obstructing Mr Stolliams's view. Luckily, because there hadn't been any music, he didn't notice.

I played the song and Joppin jogged eagerly, causing a laugh. Then, at the end of the song, I did the bubble trick. Everyone cheered and a few small kids ran about trying to pop the bubbles as they floated across the café. Joppin then did a drum roll on a small toy drum. Everyone was waiting for the underpants to fly out. Joppin then started loading the pants into the trumpet.

'What on earth?' shouted a shocked voice from the audience. Mr Stolliams had a large paper bag on his head and his arms were flailing around as he tried to take it off.

I blew like mad. The pants dropped out pathetically onto the floor. Everyone began cheering. Mr Stolliams eventually got the bag off his head and looked around furiously. Mandy pointed at baby Bobo who was sitting on Sarah's knee. Mr Stolliams shook his head in despair. Sarah looked very embarrassed. Mandy smiled at me.

Yippee. Mr Stolliams hadn't seen any underpants at all. The only unusual things he'd seen were the bubbles. He came up to me at the end. 'Have you been using washing up liquid to clean your trumpet?' he asked, he then leaned over and whispered, 'It's better to just use a trumpet cleaning brush.'

'OK,' I said innocently.

'Good concert though, well done.'

HOORAY!

(I feel a song coming on.)

Number of problems equals zero.

Number of problems equals none.

Number of problems equals zero.

All my problems are g-g-gone.

P.S. that reminds me of a joke...

What did the 0 say to the 8?

Nice belt.

Ha-ha-ha-ha!

Monday, May 20th

Claire got a dip in the lucky bag today. She got a pack of three mini highlighter pens. Nearly everyone in the class has had a dip in the bag now. Only me, Peter Potter and Rush are left. It seems that however hard I try I don't get a star. I may have to have a word with Mr Burple about this.

Monday, June 3rd

Only 19 days to go until the world record attempt. I have been practising standing on the gym ball a bit, but it is so easy peasy that I'm not too worried.

Tuesday, June 4th

We did gardening today. My area had two dandelions. Sarah said that if you touch the white liquid in a dandelion stalk, it makes you wee straight away. I had fun chasing her about with the stem. A few people now have flowers but most people just have a few shoots with the odd slug-eaten leaf.

Mr Burple was very excited about it all though. He went up to Rush and said, 'Ohhh, look a stem of a real plant. You grew that; are you proud?'

Thursday, June 6th

OH NO, Peter Potter got a dip in the lucky bag today. This just leaves Rush and me, and he's only been here half the year.

Monday, June 10th
BAD, BAD NEWS

Mr Burple said that as Rush missed part of the year he was going to give him five bonus stars. This meant that Rush got a dip in the lucky bag! There is now only one person who has not had a dip in the bag and that person is NOT very happy about it!

After lunch, I told Mr Burple that I was the only one who hadn't had a dip in the bag. He walked over with me and looked at my chart.

'Oh dear Maggie, you really need to try harder; I didn't realize how little effort you've put in this year. I'm going to move you to the front.' Oh no, next to Peter Potter, again. Aghaaaaa!

Tuesday, June 11th

Mr Burple said that we are having a money-handling lesson tomorrow. The classroom is going to become a shop for the morning. 'I will provide everything, no one needs money as I have toy money,' Mr Burple said.

'I've got £10 from my birthday; I'm bringing it just in case,' Jake whispered to Peter.

Wednesday, June 12th

Today, we had the money-handling lesson. Mr Burple had set the classroom up to look like a funny old-fashioned shop. He'd brought in lots of strange items from his house. On each item he'd put a price label. There was a big box of toy money on his desk.

This is a list of some of Mr Burple's strange items (with prices)

Dirty plastic funnel ………………….. *£1.50*

A broken clock ……………….. *£7.00*

A shopping bag made of string………… *£15.00* *(bit expensive if you ask me)*

An old radio ………………………………*£4.90*

Two chipped plates ……………….*£9*

A pot of white face powder …………*£2*

There was even more of this kind of stuff. The classroom looked like a stall at a car boot sale, the stall that everyone would walk straight past.

We were given roles of shopkeeper, buyer or browser. We then took it in turns to buy and sell things using the toy money. It was going well until Jake bought the face powder. He had a real £2 coin in his pocket and paid with that. He then insisted that the transaction was legally binding. He said his mum was a solicitor and he was sure that, in court, the sale would be seen as proper.

'Oh no, OK then,' said a worried Mr Burple. This caused huge excitement as everyone started getting cash out of their pockets.

Mr Burple looked extremely flustered, as he reluctantly had to sell all this things. (Only the shopping bag didn't sell.) I saw him sadly putting the toy money away at the end of the lesson.

I wonder what I'll do with my new dirty plastic funnel?

Friday, June 14th
TRUMPET LESSON

Mr Stolliams gave me a gift at the end of the lesson. He said it was a reward for working so hard at the trumpet this year. It was a trumpet cleaning brush. Mr Burple also gave me a star for good trumpeting progress. I now only have three more stars to go.

Saturday, June 22nd
RECORD ATTEMPT

I woke up so nervous today knowing it was the day of the world record attempt. I wore my longest t-shirt and black leggings. The reason I had to wear the longest t-shirt I could find is because I was going to be wearing, (don't tell anyone), a nappy, It was Sarah's idea. She gave me one of Bobo's nappies yesterday. This meant that if I did need a wee within the five hours and eight minutes, it would be OK. I was also being careful not to drink too much, as I didn't really want to have to 'use' the nappy.

Dad put the gym ball in the boot and we set off to school. When we got there, I couldn't believe it. There was a big van from the local TV station, and there was a large queue of people waiting to go in. There were reporters and photographers, and there were even three portable loos in the car park. All this for me and my world record attempt. I had no idea it was going to be such a big thing.

As we walked in, people took photos and asked me how I felt.

'Quite confident,' I said as I scurried in and went for another last wee.

In the hall, there was a square of red carpet on the stage. Lots of chairs filled the room and a large TV camera had been set up at the back. Dad put the ball on the stage. People started coming in and sitting down. Mum, Dad and my friends were at the front. Loads of other kids and families filled the remaining seats. I hung around at the edge of the stage.

'Hi, I'm Lula,' a woman with an American accent shook my hand. She had a clipboard, bright white teeth and loads of fluffy blonde hair. 'I'm from the World Records Society. I'll introduce you, time the event and check the ball, OK?'

'Oh, yeah,' I said, glad that someone was in charge. Lula felt the ball.

'Much too slack,' she said. She got out a bike pump with a digital display on it. She pumped up the ball. It was now much bigger and firmer. 'The ball's at the correct official pressure now,' she said. 'I'll introduce you. Are you ready?'

I nodded and did a few stretches, 'Yep, I'm ready.'

'Good morning to everyone who has come to watch this great event,' she began. 'Maggie will be standing on this ball for over five hours. I realise this is a long time for spectators so we have a buffet in classroom one, extra portable toilets outside and cushions for people to sit on. Feel free to come and go as you please.'

There was a buzz in the air; everyone seemed excited to be part of the event. I couldn't believe they were all there for me.

The photographers from the newspapers and magazines were getting ready at the front. Lula held the ball ready.

'Let's count down from five to start this off,' she said, checking her stopwatch. Everyone

counted down and I jumped on. It felt very different to usual. Incredibly hard and... impossible to stand on. I fell off after three seconds. Luckily Bobo's nappy provided a soft landing. I, however, was starting to panic. I knew I couldn't do it. It was so easy when the ball was really soft, but now there was no chance.

'Oh dear,' said Lula helping me up. 'Don't worry, we'll count down again, from five.'

Everyone counted down from five. I jumped on and lasted... one second. I could feel the nappy bunching up near the top of my leggings. This put me off even more.

'Oh, um, you're allowed three attempts,' said Lula, looking worried.

'Count down from three.'

I lasted half a second and fell face first over the ball. I knew there'd be a big trouser bulge facing the audience so I slid forward down the ball and lay on the floor out of view. The photographers shook their heads and left the room. Everyone in the audience started mumbling. Lula suggested I go out to get a drink. I rushed out, mortified. When I crept back in, everyone was leaving. We drove home in silence.

Oh dear.

Monday, June 24th

Everyone at school was asking me what happened. It was so embarrassing. I pretended it was because I'd strained my toe. This meant that I had to limp all day.

I also got in trouble with Dad for trying to flush a nappy down the loo. Apparently it is very, very bad to try and flush a nappy down the loo. It also led to a rather awkward conversation.

Tuesday, June 25th

I'm still pretending to limp. (When I remember.)

We went to look at our gardening plots today. Guess what! I have about six poppies. Mr Burple was extremely excited about this and he gave me two good work stars! This means I only have one more to get. This is good news because there are only a few more weeks until the summer holidays.

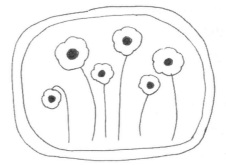

We looked round everyone's plots. They all looked pretty ropey. Holly had absolutely nothing, just slug trails. Sarah had a few shoots and Mandy had a garden gnome that she's brought in but not much else. Peter was off ill but his plot has loads of strange plants that looked like hay and weird long grasses. Not quite the one flower and one pebble garden he had planned.

Suddenly Quentin started shouting, 'Yes, yes!' We went over to see what the fuss was about. To everyone's astonishment there, lying on the soil within his plot, were about eight huge, shiny purple aubergines.

Mr Burple sprinted over and Quentin handed him one of the aubergines. He looked at it like it was the most amazing thing he had ever seen. His mouth fell open as he gently rubbed it.

'This shows you children what is possible in this life,' he said. 'From a few tiny seeds many great aubergines have grown. You are like the seeds, you too could become aubergines.'

Jake started giggling. Quentin looked at him and flicked his hair dramatically; he then put the aubergines into two plastic bags. A large, smug smile filled his face. 'Yes, I am naturally good at growing,' he told everyone as we filed back into the classroom. 'My mind and my aubergines grow exceptionally well.'

When we got back into the classroom I put the stars on my star chart and Quentin put the aubergines under his desk.

'Well Quentin,' said Mr Burple. 'I think you'll be getting the best gardener prize trophy this year. We need to wait another two weeks though in case anyone else surprises me.' We all knew that no one else would be surprising him.

MATHS LESSON

We did funny brainteasers today. Here is one that Mr Burple wrote on the board.

'If there are three bananas and you take away two bananas how many do you have?'

We all said one but Mr Burple said, 'No... If you take away two bananas then of course you have two.' He was chuckling away to himself.

He rubbed it out and wrote another one on the white board.

'What occurs once in every minute, twice in every moment but never in a thousand years?'

Jake thought it was burping. He was wrong. Mr Burple could hardly contain himself as he told us the answer. 'The letter 'M' of course,' he said, pointing to all the M's on the board.

ASSEMBLY

In assembly, Mr Burple showed everyone in the school the aubergines. Mrs Foley was particularly impressed and even put her glasses on to take a closer look. She said that because of his spectacular vegetables she was going to be giving the gardening trophy out early. Quentin walked up to receive the trophy. He put one of the aubergines in it and held it up.

QUENTIN'S SPEECH

'Thank you all for being here while I receive this trophy. Some people are naturally good at things. I am lucky to be one of those people. If anyone ever needs any help with anything, please let me know.'

We were all getting sick of Quentin.

After assembly, we went back to our classroom and did quiet reading. Quentin put the trophy on his desk and the bags of aubergines under his desk. We read for about five minutes then....

KNOCK, KNOCK, KNOCK.

Someone was knocking on the door urgently. We all looked up in alarm. In walked Mrs Foley and Quentin's dad. He looked very cross in his apron, his hands on his hips. The colour drained out of Quentin's face. Mrs Foley walked up to Quentin. She bent down, her nose was very near his.

'It seems there has been a misunderstanding,' she said, looking closely at him.

'Oh?' muttered Quentin. Quentin's dad stepped forward.

'Why did you take my aubergines from the kitchen this morning?' he shouted. 'I got them from the market yesterday for a dinner party I'm cooking for tonight!' He took a deep breath. 'I went to the cupboard today and what did I find? A note saying 'I've borrowed your aubergines for the day, from Quentin'.' He looked like he might burst. 'What kind of person borrows aubergines for the day?'

Mrs Foley plucked the trophy from Quentin's desk and stood holding it for a long moment. Silence swirled around. 'The gardening contest is still open,' she said eventually. They both left; Quentin's dad grabbed the bags of aubergines from under Quentin's desk on the way out.

We all pretended to continue our quiet reading but everyone was giggling. Quentin shook his head. 'I did grow them,' he said, 'then I took them to the market where Dad bought them.'

Everyone laughed.

Friday, June 28th

Mandy and I both have July birthdays so we have decided to have a joint party. We are going to the cinema then to a restaurant for pizza. The party is in two weeks, on Saturday, 13 July. Mum is buying me a new outfit as part of my present. First of all she said I could wear my tablecloth dress, then she tried to fob me off with some old-fashioned dresses from her eBay shop, but I didn't like them so we are going to town this Saturday. Yippee.

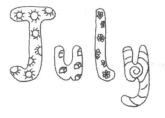

Saturday, July 6th

I had a nice day in town with Mum. I got my outfit... dark denim jeans and a black and purple stripy t-shirt. After that we went for a cup of tea and a slice of cake. Then it was time to get Mandy a present. We spent ages in W.H. Smiths. I managed to steer Mum away from the maths and literacy books and picked a really nice pencil case with a gold and silver pen in it. I also got some black paper and envelopes to go with it. She will love it.

Friday, July 12th

Birthday and cinema party tomorrow! We are seeing 'My Hamster is an Alien'. We have to go really early though because the cinema is running a superhero convention at the same time. There will be lots of people dressed up and there are loads of superhero films on so it could be busy. It will be funny seeing all the costumes. Our film is the only one that is not about superheroes.

Saturday, July 13th
BIRTHDAY
Morning:

Whoopie doo! Today is my birthday. I got up mega early and waited downstairs on my own for ages. There were three oddly shaped presents on the rug. I spent a while trying to work out what they were.

When Mum, Dad and Joppin came down, I excitedly went to get the presents but Mum said I had to have breakfast first. I had the world's fastest breakfast. (Perhaps that should have been my record attempt.) Then I opened the first present. It said 'Made with love, from Dad' on the tag.

I opened it. Inside was a wooden box with a stick coming out of the top. On the end of the stick was an inflated yellow rubber glove.

'What is it?' I asked.

'An automatic waver; go on, give it a go.'

I pushed the glove and the stick moved back and forth, kind of giving the impression of a wave.

'Thanks Dad, it's great,' I said, hoping that the next present would be better.

I looked at the tag. It said 'Handmade with love, from Mum.' Oh dear, it was not going as well as I'd hoped. I opened Mum's present. It was a metal coat hanger with a strange patchwork bag hanging from it. 'It's a pyjama bag darling, made from scraps of clothes I couldn't sell. It's for the back of your door. Dad's already put a hook up.'

'Thanks Mum,' I said, despairing that I'd have to put it on my door and look at it every day. Last was Joppin's gift. I looked nervously at the tag and yes, my worst fear was confirmed. It said 'Handmade by Joppin'. I opened it, it was a long stick with the other yellow rubber glove stuffed and stuck on the end. Some of the fingers were tied down with a rubber band so it looked a bit like it was pointing.

'It's a pointer,' said Joppin excitedly, 'for when you're too far away from something to point at it. It gives you an extra 70 centimetres.'

'Thanks Joppin,' I said. I was trying not to sound too fed up.

All the handmade presents were kind of terrible. In a way they were worse than no presents as they'll clutter up my room and I won't be able to throw them away for ages.

Well at least I'll get presents from my friends when we meet up later. I'll update about the party and presents when I get back.

P.S. I think Mandy may have got me something from America.

Afternoon: PARTY NEWS!

Well I had a very embarrassing car ride to the cinema. Because I'd pretended to like Dad's present he'd insisting on putting it in the car. It was jammed between the window and me. I looked straight ahead as the yellow hand waved insanely at passers-by. Even worse, because there wasn't much room in the car, the horrible rubber glove repeatedly hit me in the face with each wave.

Joppin had also said that I could take his rubber glove pointing stick out. Mum said that as Joppin had put so much effort into making it, taking it would be the right thing to do. This meant that as we left the car and went to the cinema I had to carry a horrible smelly glove on a stick with me. I hid the stick down my new jeans. I told Joppin that I had a special long pocket and he seemed to believe me. It meant that the yellow glove was coming out of the leg of my jeans like a horrible yellow foot. I heard a woman saying 'Oh did you see that poor girl's foot?' as she ushered her children away from me.

Because the stick was down my trousers, I couldn't bend my leg. This meant I walked oddly and drew even more attention to myself.

We went into the cinema to meet the others. Because of the superhero convention there were people dressed up everywhere. Lots of people were in Superman, Spiderman and Batman outfits. There were also loads of superheroes I hadn't heard off and I think some people had made up their own.

Someone asked me if I was Super Rancid Toes, I rushed away.

Just after that I saw a man in a skin-tight pink body suit with purple underpants over the top. He had a purple cape and mask on too. He looked very familiar. It was … Mr Stolliams. I stared at him, catching his eye. He stared at me for a moment, looking startled, then vanished behind a post. My goodness!

'Maggie, Maggie,' It was my friends calling me. I hobbled over to them and we went to see the film. I tried to get the pointing stick out but it was stuck. I had to watch the whole film with my leg very straight. Not that comfy.

The film was good. The hamster alien spoke perfect English and there were lots of jokes about the facilities in the cage. After the film, I limped past various superheroes as we made our way to the restaurant.

THE MEAL

Yum.... The pizza was good. This man came along with a guitar and played Happy Birthday to Mandy and me. I had to put my face in my hands until it was over. Other people we didn't know were joining in.

We decided to do the present exchange over desert. (Chocolate cake and ice cream for me.)

Mandy opened her gifts first. She loved the pencil case and metallic pens.

Then I opened my presents. I got.....

A '100 sums a day' book from Sarah

A stuffed sock with button eyes from Holly (Worm's baby apparently)

A turnip from Mandy

They were all in hysterics.

'We know you like to do joke presents,' said Holly.

'Sorry,' said Mandy, 'I really thought you'd be getting me a joke present so I got you one.' She looked a bit embarrassed and offered me the silver pen. I took it.

So here I am, back at home looking at my gifts. My room looks terrible with rubber gloves waving,

turnips smelling, stuffed socks laughing, messy
pointers pointing, pyjama case hanging and maths
book looming.

Wednesday, July 17th

The rubber glove started waving in the middle
of the night. It squeaked horribly with each wave
and woke me up. I managed to stop it by jamming
the stuffed sock into it.

Friday, July 19th

Last trumpet lesson of term today. I was going
to ask Mr Stolliams about his superhero costume. I
was just about to speak when he said, 'I was
nowhere near any cinema on Saturday. In fact I

was at a debating club meeting for the philosophy society.' Hmm.

We are going to be playing a song for the end-of-term assembly on Friday. It's a song called 'Somewhere Over The Rainbow'. It's meant to be quite slow but for some reason Rush plays it really fast. He's finished the whole song before everyone else is even on the third line. Because of this, it doesn't sound that good. Rush says it's meant to be fast. Mr Stolliams just shakes his head in despair. Mr Burple even got on one knee to beg him to slow down.

'You'll wear out your knee patches doing that,' said Quentin.

Mr Burple got up quickly.

It was also Mandy's birthday today so we sang to her and she described all the presents she got from her family. They sounded really good.

Mandy's presents:

Pencil with electric rubber that spins when you press a button

Roller skates

Games system

Hamster with 'palace' habitat

Four tops, two pairs of jeans and two pairs of trainers

Bedroom makeover

Sixteen new rubbers for her collection – all proper shapes

I wonder if there's a way I can permanently lock up Dad's workshop.

Monday, July 22nd

Only today and tomorrow left then it's the summer holidays. Today, we did this thing called the 'Review of the year'. We had to talk about how the year went. Mr Burple had this idea that we should all write a poem called 'What I've learnt this year'.

I wrote...

What I've learnt this year

By Maggie Moore

Mr Burple isn't purple (although he's been close a couple of times)

People like to laugh (usually at me)

Nothing hard is secretly easy

Embarrassing feelings pass (a bit)

And guess what! I got a good work star for it. This meant that I finally got a dip in the lucky bag. Yes, I was the last person in the class but at that moment I was on top of the world. It was like everything I'd been working for all year had come together. I wouldn't have worked anything like so hard if it weren't for the thought of that lucky dip bag.

I, like the 29 children before me, excitedly walked up to the front. Mr Burple got out the special purple bag. I put my shaking hand in and

felt about. I felt...nothing. I felt about a bit more...a few crumbs. I had one last feel about and found something. It was small, rectangular and smooth. I pulled it out. It was a small, plain white grubby rubber covered in pencil sharpenings. I hid

it in my pocket and went back to my desk, hoping
no one would ask me what it was.

'What is it?' asked Mandy.

Tuesday, July 23rd
LAST DAY OF TERM

We had the end of term assembly today.
Various awards and certificates were given out.

Mrs Foley had put a big whiteboard at the front
of the hall and photos of people's achievements
were being shown. I was in one of them. Well,
there was a clear of view of the side of the tuffet
underneath Claire.

Mrs Foley held up the gardening trophy. A
photo of a garden full of all sorts of different-
coloured flowers came up on the screen. No one
could believe any of us could have grown such a
good garden.

'Gardener of the year trophy goes to the child
who created this garden,' said Mrs Foley, pointing
at the photo. 'Peter Potter, please come up.'

Peter looked up, his mouth open wide. He went
up to the front of the hall and everyone cheered

as he took the trophy. Quentin frowned and mumbled that it should have been his.

At the end of assembly we did the trumpet performance. I was a bit nervous because of Rush but, amazingly, it actually sounded good. You could hardly hear Rush at all. I knew that dirty funnel would come in handy.

After the song, Mr Burple shed a few tears of happiness as he'd finally played music in public. Mrs Foley suggested he sit quietly in the staff room, so he shuffled off.

Friday, July 26th

So that's it, another school year over. The rain is beating down on the window, thunder is rolling in the sky and I am packing ready for camping tomorrow...

HAPPY SUMMER!
THE END

Also available

6509238R00106

Printed in Germany
by Amazon Distribution
GmbH, Leipzig